Read ALL the

THE CAT WHO COULD ~~___~~ mystery to many-~~____~~ ~~____~~ to a mystery of ano~~____~~

THE CAT WHO A ~~____~~ covering the inte~~____~~ murderer has de~~____~~ stories . . .

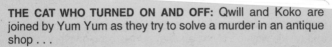

Fort Lupton
Public & School Library
425 S. Denver Ave.
Fort Lupton, CO 80621
fortluptonlibrary.org
303-857-7180

THE CAT WHO TURNED ON AND OFF: Qwill and Koko are joined by Yum Yum as they try to solve a murder in an antique shop . . .

THE CAT WHO SAW RED: Qwill starts his diet—and a new gourmet column for the *Fluxion*. It isn't easy—but it's not as hard as solving a shocking murder case . . .

THE CAT WHO PLAYED BRAHMS: While fishing at a secluded cabin, Qwill hooks onto a murder mystery—and Koko gets hooked on classical music . . .

THE CAT WHO PLAYED POST OFFICE: Koko and Yum Yum turn into fat cats when Qwill inherits millions. But amid the caviar and champagne, Koko smells something fishy . . .

THE CAT WHO KNEW SHAKESPEARE: The local newspaper publisher has perished in an accident—or is it murder? That is the question . . .

THE CAT WHO SNIFFED GLUE: After a rich banker and his wife are killed, Koko develops an odd appetite for glue. To solve the murder, Qwill has to figure out why . . .

THE CAT WHO WENT UNDERGROUND: Qwill and the cats head for their Moose County cabin to relax—but when a handyman disappears, Koko must dig up some clues . . .

THE CAT WHO TALKED TO GHOSTS: Qwill and Koko try to solve a haunting mystery in a historic farmhouse . . .

continued . . .

THE CAT WHO LIVED HIGH: A glamorous art dealer was killed in Qwill's high-rise—and he and the cats reach new heights in detection as they try to solve the case . . .

THE CAT WHO KNEW A CARDINAL: The director of the local Shakespeare production dies in Qwill's orchard—and the stage is set for a puzzling mystery . . .

THE CAT WHO MOVED A MOUNTAIN: Qwill moves to the beautiful Potato Mountains—where a dispute between residents and developers boils over into murder . . .

THE CAT WHO WASN'T THERE: Qwill's on his way to Scotland—and on his way to solving another purr-plexing mystery . . .

THE CAT WHO WENT INTO THE CLOSET: Qwill's moved into a mansion . . . with fifty closets for Koko to investigate! But among the junk, Koko finds a clue . . .

THE CAT WHO CAME TO BREAKFAST: Qwill and the cats scramble for clues when peaceful Breakfast Island is turned upside down by real-estate developers, controversy—and murder . . .

THE CAT WHO BLEW THE WHISTLE: An old steam locomotive has been restored, causing excitement in Moose County. But murder brings the fun to a screeching halt . . .

THE CAT WHO SAID CHEESE: At the Great Food Explo, scheduled events include a bake-off, a cheese tasting, and a restaurant opening. Unscheduled events include mystery and murder . . .

THE CAT WHO TAILED A THIEF: A rash of petty thievery and a wealthy woman's death leave a trail of clues as elusive as a cat burglar . . .

THE CAT WHO SANG FOR THE BIRDS: Spring comes to Moose County—and a young cat's fancy turns to crime solving . . .

THE CAT WHO SAW STARS: UFOs in Mooseville? When a backpacker disappears, Qwill investigates a rumored "abduction"—with the help of his own little aliens . . .

THE CAT WHO ROBBED A BANK: As the Highland Games approach, Qwill tries to make sense of Koko's sudden interest in photographs, pennies, and paper towels . . .

THE CAT WHO SMELLED A RAT: A drought plagues Moose County—and a bewildering murder case plagues Qwill and the cats . . .

THE CAT WHO WENT UP THE CREEK: While visiting Black Creek, Qwill and the cats must solve the murder of a drowned man before they're up the creek without a paddle . . .

THE CAT WHO BROUGHT DOWN THE HOUSE: Koko's stage debut is postponed when Qwill suspects the cat's costar may be guilty of murder . . .

THE CAT WHO TALKED TURKEY: A body's been found on Qwill's property, and now he and the cats will have to determine who committed this fowl deed . . .

THE CAT WHO WENT BANANAS: Koko finds a bunch of clues when an out-of-town actor dies mysteriously . . .

THE CAT WHO DROPPED A BOMBSHELL: As Pickax plans its big parade, Qwill and the cats cope with an approaching storm—and two suspicious deaths . . .

THE CAT WHO HAD 60 WHISKERS: News of a fatal bee sting has Koko's whiskers twitching—and Qwill itching to find out more . . .

And don't miss . . .

THE CAT WHO HAD 14 TALES: A delightful collection of feline mystery fiction!

SHORT & TALL TALES: LEGENDS OF MOOSE COUNTY
Legends, stories, and anecdotes from four hundred miles north of everywhere . . .

THE PRIVATE LIFE OF THE CAT WHO . . .
A charming collection of feline antics that provides an intimate look at the private lives of those extraordinary Siamese cats Koko and Yum Yum.

Titles by Lilian Jackson Braun

THE CAT WHO COULD READ BACKWARDS
THE CAT WHO ATE DANISH MODERN
THE CAT WHO TURNED ON AND OFF
THE CAT WHO SAW RED
THE CAT WHO PLAYED BRAHMS
THE CAT WHO PLAYED POST OFFICE
THE CAT WHO KNEW SHAKESPEARE
THE CAT WHO SNIFFED GLUE
THE CAT WHO WENT UNDERGROUND
THE CAT WHO TALKED TO GHOSTS
THE CAT WHO LIVED HIGH
THE CAT WHO KNEW A CARDINAL
THE CAT WHO MOVED A MOUNTAIN
THE CAT WHO WASN'T THERE
THE CAT WHO WENT INTO THE CLOSET
THE CAT WHO CAME TO BREAKFAST
THE CAT WHO BLEW THE WHISTLE
THE CAT WHO SAID CHEESE
THE CAT WHO TAILED A THIEF
THE CAT WHO SANG FOR THE BIRDS
THE CAT WHO SAW STARS
THE CAT WHO ROBBED A BANK
THE CAT WHO SMELLED A RAT
THE CAT WHO WENT UP THE CREEK
THE CAT WHO BROUGHT DOWN THE HOUSE
THE CAT WHO TALKED TURKEY
THE CAT WHO WENT BANANAS
THE CAT WHO DROPPED A BOMBSHELL
THE CAT WHO HAD 60 WHISKERS

SHORT STORY COLLECTIONS:
THE CAT WHO HAD 14 TALES
SHORT & TALL TALES
THE PRIVATE LIFE OF THE CAT WHO...

Lilian Jackson Braun

The Cat Who Knew Shake- speare

J

JOVE BOOKS, NEW YORK

THE BERKLEY PUBLISHING GROUP
Published by the Penguin Group
Penguin Group (USA) Inc.
375 Hudson Street, New York, New York 10014, USA
Penguin Group (Canada), 90 Eglinton Avenue East, Suite 700, Toronto, Ontario M4P 2Y3, Canada
(a division of Pearson Penguin Canada Inc.)
Penguin Books Ltd., 80 Strand, London WC2R 0RL, England
Penguin Group Ireland, 25 St. Stephen's Green, Dublin 2, Ireland (a division of Penguin Books Ltd.)
Penguin Group (Australia), 250 Camberwell Road, Camberwell, Victoria 3124, Australia
(a division of Pearson Australia Group Pty. Ltd.)
Penguin Books India Pvt. Ltd., 11 Community Centre, Panchsheel Park, New Delhi—110 017, India
Penguin Group (NZ), 67 Apollo Drive, Rosedale, North Shore 0632, New Zealand
(a division of Pearson New Zealand Ltd.)
Penguin Books (South Africa) (Pty.) Ltd., 24 Sturdee Avenue, Rosebank, Johannesburg 2196,
South Africa

Penguin Books Ltd., Registered Offices: 80 Strand, London WC2R 0RL, England

This is a work of fiction. Names, characters, places, and incidents either are the product of the author's imagination or are used fictitiously, and any resemblance to actual persons, living or dead, business establishments, events, or locales is entirely coincidental. The publisher does not have any control over and does not assume any responsibility for author or third-party websites or their content.

THE CAT WHO KNEW SHAKESPEARE

A Jove Book / published by arrangement with the author

PRINTING HISTORY
First Jove mass-market edition / June 1988

ISBN: 978-0-515-09582-1

JOVE®
Jove Books are published by The Berkley Publishing Group,
a division of Penguin Group (USA) Inc.,
375 Hudson Street, New York, New York 10014.
JOVE and the "J" design are trademarks belonging to Penguin Group (USA) Inc.

PRINTED IN THE UNITED STATES OF AMERICA

43   42   41

ONE

In Moose County, four hundred miles north of everywhere, it always starts to snow in November, and it snows—and snows—and snows.

First, all the front steps disappear under two feet of snow. Then fences and shrubs are no longer visible. Utility poles keep getting shorter until the lines are low enough for limbo dancing. Listening to the hourly weather reports on the radio is everyone's winter hobby in Moose County, and snowplowing becomes the chief industry. Plows and blowers throw up mountains of white that hide whole buildings and require the occupants to tunnel through to the street. In Pickax City, the county seat, it's not unusual to see cross-country skis in the downtown shopping area. If the airport closes down—and it often does—Moose County is an island of snow and ice. It all starts in November, with a storm that the residents call the Big One.

On the evening of November fifth, Jim Qwilleran was relaxing in his comfortable library in the company of friends. A mood of contentment prevailed. They had dined well, the housekeeper having prepared clam chowder and escalopes of veal Casimir. The houseman had piled fragrant logs of applewood in the fireplace, and the blaze projected dancing highlights on the leather-bound books that filled four walls of library shelves. From softly shaded lamps came a golden glow that warmed the leather furniture and Bokhara rugs.

Qwilleran, a large middle-aged man with a bushy moustache, sat at his antique English desk and tuned in the nine o'clock weather report on the radio—one of numerous small portables deployed about the house for this purpose.

"Colder tonight, with lows about twenty-five degrees," the WPKX meteorologist predicted. "High winds and a good chance of snow tonight and tomorrow."

Qwilleran flipped off the radio. "If you guys don't object," he said to the other two, "I'd like to leave town for a few days. It's six months since my last trip Down Below, and my cronies at the newspaper think I'm dead. Mrs. Cobb will serve your meals, and I'll be back before the snow flies—I hope. Just keep your paws crossed."

Four brown ears swiveled alertly at the announcement. Two brown masks with long white whiskers and incredibly blue eyes turned away from the blazing logs and toward the man seated at the desk.

The more you talk to cats, Qwilleran had been told, the smarter they become. An occasional "nice kitty" will have no measurable effect; intelligent conversation is required.

The system, he had found, seemed to be working; the pair of Siamese on the hearth rug reacted as if they knew exactly what he was saying. Yum Yum, the affectionate little female, gazed at him with an expression that looked like reproach. Koko, the handsome and muscular male, rose from the spot where he had been lounging in leonine majesty, walked stiffly to the desk, and scolded with earsplitting yowls. "Yow-ow-OW!"

"I was expecting a little more understanding and consideration," the man told them.

Qwilleran, at the age of fifty or so, was coping with a unique midlife crisis. After a lifetime of living in large metropolitan areas, he was now a resident of Pickax City, population 3,000. After a career as a hardworking journalist getting by with a modest salary, he was now a millionaire—or billionaire; he was not quite sure. At any rate, he was the sole heir to the Klingenschoen fortune founded in Moose County in the nineteenth century. The bequest included a mansion on Main Street, a staff of three, a four-car garage, and a limousine. Even after a year or more he found his new lifestyle strange. As a newsman he had been concerned chiefly with getting the story, checking the facts, meeting the deadline, and protecting his sources. Now his chief concern, like that of every other Moose County adult, seemed to be the weather, especially in November.

When the Siamese reacted negatively to his proposal, Qwilleran tamped his moustache thoughtfully for a moment. "Nevertheless," he said, "it's imperative that I go. Arch Riker is leaving the *Daily Fluxion*, and I'm hosting his retirement party Friday night."

In his days of frugal bachelorhood in a one-room apartment, Qwilleran had never hungered for money or possessions, and among his fellow staffers he was not noted for his generosity. But when the Klingenschoen estate finally stumbled through probate court, he astonished the media of the Western world by inviting the entire staff of the *Daily Fluxion* to a dinner at the Press Club.

He planned to take a guest: Junior Goodwinter, the young managing editor of the *Pickax Picayune*, Moose County's only newspaper. Dialing the newspaper office, he said, "Hi, Junior! How would you like to goof off for a couple of days and fly Down Below for a party? My treat. Cocktails and dinner at the Press Club."

"Oh, wow! I've never seen a Press Club except in

the movies," said the editor. "Could we visit the *Daily Fluxion* offices, too?"

Junior looked and dressed like a high school sophomore and exhibited an innocent enthusiasm that was rare in a journalist with a *cum laude* degree from a state university.

"We might sneak in a hockey game and a couple of shows, too," Qwilleran said, "but we'll have to keep an eye on the weather reports and get back here before snow flies."

"There's a low-pressure front moving down from Canada, but I think we're safe for a while," Junior said. "What's the party all about?"

"A retirement bash for Arch Riker, and here's what I want you to do: Bring a *Picayune* newscarrier's sack and a hundred copies of your latest issue. After the dinner I'll say a few words about Moose County and the *Picayune*, and that'll be your cue to jump up and start distributing the papers."

"I'll wear a baseball cap sideways and yell, 'Extra! Extra!' Is that what you want?"

"You've got it!" Qwilleran said. "But the authentic pronunciation is 'Wuxtree!' Be ready at nine o'clock Friday morning. I'll pick you up at your office."

The early-morning weather broadcast on Friday was not encouraging: "A low-pressure front hovering over Canada increases the possibility of heavy snow tonight and tomorrow, with winds shifting to the northeast."

Qwilleran's housekeeper expressed her fears.

"What will you do, Mr. Q, if you can't get back here before snow flies? If the storm is the Big One, the airport will be closed for goodness knows how long."

"Well, I'll tell you, Mrs. Cobb. I'll rent a dogsled and a pack of huskies and mush back to Pickax."

"Oh, Mr. Q!" she laughed. "I never know whether to believe you or not."

She was preparing an attractive plate of sautéed chicken livers with a garnish of hard-cooked egg yolk and bacon crumbles, which she placed on the floor. Yum Yum gobbled her share hungrily, but Koko declined to eat. Something was bothering him.

Both cats had the shaded fawn bodies and brown points of pedigreed seal-point Siamese: brown masks accentuating the blueness of their eyes; alert brown ears worn like royal crowns; brown legs elegantly long and slender; brown tails that lashed and curled and waved to express emotions and opinions. But Koko had something more: a disconcerting degree of intelligence and an uncanny knack of knowing when something was . . . *wrong*!

That morning he had knocked a book off a shelf in the library.

"That's bad form!" Qwilleran had told him, appealing to his intelligence. "These are old, rare, and valuable books—to be treated with respect, if not reverence." He examined the book. It was a slender leather-bound copy of *The Tempest*—one of a thirty-seven-volume set of Shakespeare's plays that had come with the house.

Experiencing slight qualms, Qwilleran replaced the book on the shelf. It was an unfortunate choice of title. He was determined, however, to fly Down Below for the party, despite Koko and Mrs. Cobb and the WPKX meteorologist.

An hour before flight time he drove his energy-efficient compact to the office of the *Picayune* to pick up Junior and the sack of newspapers. All the buildings on Main Street were more than a century old, constructed of gray stone in a variety of inappropriate architectural styles. The *Picayune* headquarters—squeezed between the imitation Viennese lodge hall and the imitation Roman post office—resembled an ancient Spanish monastery.

A satisfying smell of ink pervaded the newspaper office, but the premises had the embalmed look of a museum. There was no ad taker at the scarred front counter. There was no alert and smiling receptionist—only a bell to ring for service.

Qwilleran perused the silent scene: wooden filing cabinets and well-worn desks of golden oak . . . dangerous-looking spindles for spiking ad orders and subscriptions . . . old copies of the *Picayune*, yellow and brittle, plastered on walls that had not been painted since the Great Depression. Beyond the low partition of golden oak and unwashed glass was the composing room. A lone man stood before the typecases, oblivious to everything except the line of type he was setting with darting movements of his hand.

Unlike the *Daily Fluxion*, which had a metropol-

itan circulation approaching a million, the anti-
quated presses of the *Picayune* clanked out thirty-
two hundred copies of each issue. While the *Fluxion*
adopted every technological advance and journalis-
tic trend, the *Picayune* still resembled the newspaper
founded by Junior's great-grandfather. Four pages,
printed from hand-set type, carried classified ads
and social gossip on the front page. Pancake breakfasts, ice cream socials, and funerals were covered in
depth, while brief mentions of local politics, police
news, and accidents were relegated to the back page
or omitted entirely.

Qwilleran banged his fist on the bell, and Junior
Goodwinter came pelting down the wooden stairs
from the editorial office above, followed by a large
white cat.

"Who's your well-fed friend?" Qwilleran asked.

"He's William Allen, our staff mouser," said Junior casually, as if all newspapers had a mouser on
the staff.

As managing editor he wrote most of the copy
and sold most of the ads. Senior Goodwinter, owner
and publisher, spent his time in the composing
room, wearing a leather apron and a square paper
hat folded from newsprint, setting foundry type in a
composing stick while wearing an expression of
concentration and rapture. He had been setting type
since the age of eight.

Junior called out to him, "S'long, Dad. Back in a
few days."

The preoccupied man in the composing room

turned and said kindly, "Have a good time, Junior, and be careful."

"If you want to drive my Jag while I'm gone, the keys are on my desk."

"Thanks, Son, but I don't think I'll need it. The garage said my car should be ready by five o'clock. Be careful, now."

"Okay, Dad, and you take care!"

A look of warmth and mutual appreciation passed between the two, and Qwilleran momentarily regretted that he had never had a son. He would have wanted one exactly like Junior. But perhaps a little taller and a little huskier.

Junior grabbed a sack of newspapers and his duffel bag, and the two men drove to the airport. Together they were a study in generation gap: Qwilleran a sober-faced man with graying hair, luxuriant moustache, and mournful eyes; Junior a fresh-faced excited kid in running shoes. Junior opened the conversation with an abrupt question:

"Do you think I look too young, Qwill?"

"Too young for what?"

"I mean, Jody thinks no one will ever take me seriously."

"With your build and your youthful face, you'll still look like fourteen when you're seventy-five," Qwilleran told him, "and that's not all bad. After that, you'll change overnight and suddenly look like a hundred and two."

"Jody thinks it would help if I grew a beard."

"Not a bad idea! Your girl comes up with some good ones."

"My grandmother says I'd look like one of the Seven Dwarfs."

"Your grandmother sounds like a sweet person, Junior."

"Grandma Gage is a character! My mother's mother, you know. You must have seen her around town. She drives a Mercedes and honks the horn at every intersection."

Qwilleran showed no surprise. He had learned that longtime residents of Moose County were militant individualists.

"Have you heard from Melinda since she left Pickax?" Junior asked.

"A couple of times. They keep her pretty busy at the hospital. She'll be better off in Boston. She'll be able to specialize."

"Melinda never really wanted to be a country doctor, but she was hot to marry you, Qwill, and move into your mansion."

"Sorry, I'm not good husband material. I discovered that once before, and it wouldn't be fair to Melinda to make the same mistake again. I hope she meets a good man her own age in Boston."

"I hear you've got something going with the head librarian now."

Qwilleran huffed into his pepper-and-salt moustache. "I don't know what your picturesque expression implies, but let me state that I enjoy Mrs. Duncan's company. In this age of video-everything, it's good to meet someone who shares my interest in literature. We get together and read aloud."

"Oh, sure," said the younger man with a wide grin.

"When are you and Jody thinking of marrying?"

"On the salary Dad pays me I can't even afford an apartment of my own. I'm still living with my parents at the farmhouse, you know. Jody makes twice what I do, and she's only a dental hygienist."

"But you own a Jaguar."

"That was a graduation present from Grandma Gage. She's the only one in the family with dough anymore. I'll inherit when she goes, but it won't be soon. At eighty-two she still stands on her head every day, and she can beat me at push-ups. People in Moose County live a long time, barring accident. One of my ancestors was killed when his horse was spooked by a big flock of blackbirds. My Grandpa Gage was struck by lightning. I had an aunt and uncle that were killed when their car hit a deer. It was November—rutting season, you know—and this eight-point buck went right through the windshield. The sheriff said it looked like an amateur ax murder. Right now, according to official estimates, there are ten thousand deer in this county."

Qwilleran slowed his speed and started looking for signs of wildlife.

"It's bow-and-arrow season, and the hunters are making them nervous," Junior went on. "Early morning or dusk—that's when the deer bound across the highway."

"All ten thousand of them?" Qwilleran reduced his speed to forty-five.

"It sure is a gloomy day," Junior observed. "The sky looks heavy."

"What's the earliest the snow ever flies?"

"Earliest storm on record was November 2, 1919, but the Big One usually doesn't hit until midmonth. The *worst* on record was November 13, 1931. Three low-pressure fronts—from Alaska, the Rockies, and the Gulf—slammed into each other over Moose County. Lots of people lost their way in the whiteout and froze to death. When the Big One hits, you better stay indoors! Of if you're caught driving, don't get out of the car."

Despite the hazards of the north country, Qwilleran was beginning to envy the natives. They had roots! Families like the Goodwinters went back five generations—to the time when fortunes were being made in mining and lumbering. The most vital organizations in Pickax were the Historical Society and the Genealogical Club. On the Airport Road, history was unreeling: abandoned shaft houses and slag heaps at the old mine sites . . . ghost towns identifiable only by a few lonely stone chimneys . . . a crumbling railroad depot in the middle of nowhere . . . the stark remains of trees blackened by forest fires.

After a few minutes of silence Qwilleran ventured to ask Junior a personal question. "As a graduate of J-school, *cum laude*, how do you feel about the *Picayune*? Are you living up to your potential? Do you think it's right to hang back in the nineteenth century?"

"Are you kidding? My ambition is to make the *Pic* into a real newspaper," Junior said, "but Dad wants to keep it like it was a hundred years ago. He was counting on us kids to keep up the tradition, but my brother went out to California and got into advertising, and my sister married a rancher in Montana, so I'm stuck with it."

"The county could support a real newspaper. Why not start one and let your father keep the *Picayune* as a hobby? You wouldn't be competing; the *Pic* is in a class by itself. Did you ever consider anything like that?"

Junior threw him a look of panic, and the words tumbled out. "I couldn't afford to start a lemonade stand! We're broke! That's why I'm working for peanuts. . . . Every year we go further in the hole. Dad's been selling our farmland, and now he's mortgaged the farmhouse. . . . I shouldn't be telling you this. . . . Mother's been after him for a long time to unload the paper. . . . She's really upset! But Dad won't listen. He keeps right on setting type and going deeper in the red. He says it's his life—his reason for living. . . . Did you ever see him set type? He can set more than thirty-five letters a minute without looking at the typecase." Junior's face reflected his admiration.

"Yes, I've watched him, and I'm impressed," Qwilleran said. "I've also seen your presses in the basement. Some of the equipment looks like Gutenberg's winepress."

"Dad collects old presses. He has a whole barnful. My great-grandfather's first press operated with a treadle like an old sewing machine."

"Would your rich grandmother come to the rescue financially, if you wanted to start a newspaper?"

"Grandma Gage won't fork over any more dough. She's already bailed us out a couple of times and paid our insurance premiums and put three of us through college. . . . Hey, why don't you start a newspaper, Qwill? You're loaded!"

"I have absolutely no interest in or aptitude for business matters, Junior. That's why I set up the Klingenschoen Memorial Fund. They handle everything and give me a little pocket money. I spent twenty-five years on newspapers, and now all I want is the time and the quietude to do some writing."

"How's your book coming?"

"Okay," said Qwilleran, thinking of his neglected typewriter and cluttered desk and disorganized notes.

At the airport they parked in the open field that served as long-term parking lot. The terminal was little more than a shack, and the airport manager—who was also ticket agent, mechanic, and part-time pilot—was sweeping the floor. "Are we gonna get the Big One?" he asked cheerfully.

When the two newsmen boarded the twin-engine plane for the first leg of their journey, they were smart enough to avoid personal conversation. There were fifteen other passengers, and thirty ears would be listening. Moose County had a grapevine that disseminated more news than the *Picayune* and transmitted it faster than WPKX. Judiciously, Qwilleran and Junior talked about sports until the small plane bumped to a landing in Minneapolis and they boarded a jet.

"I hope they serve lunch on board," Junior said. "What are we having for dinner at the Press Club?"

"I've ordered French onion soup, prime rib, and apple pie."

"Oh, wow!"

There was a layover in Chicago before they took off on the final leg of the journey. By the time they landed and rode the coach to the Hotel Stilton and tuned in the weather reports, it was time to go to the Press Club.

"Will the sportswriters be there?" Junior asked.

"Everyone—from the top executives to the newest copyboy. I suppose they're called copy-facilitators now."

"Will they think it's corny if I ask for autographs?"

"They'll be flattered," Qwilleran said.

At the club Qwilleran was treated as a returning hero, but he reminded himself that anyone would be a hero if he staked the entire staff to dinner and an open bar. A photographer gave him a chummy poke in the ribs and asked how it felt to be a millionaire.

"I'll let you know next year, on April fifteenth," Qwilleran replied.

The travel editor wanted to know how he enjoyed living in the outback. "Isn't Moose County in the Snow Belt?"

"Absolutely! It's the buckle of the Snow Belt."

"Well, anyway, you lucky dog, you've escaped the violence of the city."

"We have plenty of violence up north," Qwilleran informed him. "Tornadoes, lightning, hurricanes, forest fires, wild animals, falling trees, spring floods! But nature's violence is easier to accept than human violence. We never have any mad snipers picking off kids on the school bus, like the incident here last week."

"Do you still have the cat that's smarter than you are?"

Around the Press Club, Qwilleran had a reputation as an amateur detective; it was also known that Koko was somewhat responsible for his success.

Qwilleran explained to Junior, "Maybe you didn't notice, but Koko's picture is hanging in the lobby, along with the Pulitzer Prize winners. Someday I'll tell you about his exploits. You won't believe it, but I'll tell you anyway."

During the happy hour Junior met the columnists and reporters whose copy he read in the outstate edition of the *Fluxion*, and he could hardly control his excitement. The guest of honor, on the other hand, was noticeably subdued. Arch Riker was glad to cut loose from the *Fluxion*, but the occasion was saddened by the recent breakup of his marriage.

"What are your plans?" Qwilleran asked.

"Well, I'll spend Thanksgiving with my son in Denver and Christmas with my daughter in Oregon. After that, I don't know."

After the prime rib and apple pie, the executive editor presented Riker with a gold watch, and Qwilleran paid a tribute to his longtime friend. He concluded with a few words about Moose County.

"Ladies and gentlemen, most of you have never heard of Moose County. It's the only underground county in the state. Cartographers sometimes forget to put it on the map. Many of our legislators think it belongs to Canada. Yet, a hundred years ago Moose County was the richest in the state, thanks to mining and lumbering. Today it's a vacation paradise for anyone interested in fishing, hunting, boating, and camping. We have two unique features I'd like to point out: perfect temperatures from May to October, and a newspaper that hasn't changed since it was founded over a century ago. Junior Goodwinter, the youngest managing editor in captivity, writes all the copy himself. In an age of satellite communication it's not easy to write with a goose quill and cuttlefish ink. . . . May I introduce Junior and the *Pickax Picayune*!"

Junior snatched his baseball cap and sack of papers and dashed about the dining room shouting, "Wuxtree! Wuxtree!" while throwing a clutch of papers on each table. The guests grabbed them and started to read—first with chuckles, then with guffaws. On page 1, in column 1, they found the classified ads:

FOR SALE: Used two-by-fours in good shape. Also a size 14 wedding dress, never been worn.

HURRY! If your old clunker won't make it through another winter, maybe you'll find a better clunker at Hackpole's Used Car Lot, or maybe you won't. Can't tell till you look 'em over.

FREE: Three gray kittens, one with white boots. Almost housebroke.

JUST ARRIVED: New shipment of long johns at Bill's Family Store. Quality ain't what it used to be, and prices are up from last year, but what the heck! Better buy before snow flies.

Sharing the front page with these examples of truth-in-advertising were news items with headlines an eighth of an inch high.

RECORD NEARLY BROKEN
   There were 75 cars in Captain Fugtree's funeral procession last week—longest since 1904, when 52 buggies and 37 carriages paraded to the cemetery to bury Ephraim Goodwinter.

BRIDAL SHOWER GIVEN
Miss Doreen Mayfus was honored at a shower last Thursday. Games were played and prizes awarded. The bride-to-be opened 24 presents. Refreshments included sausage rolls, pimiento sandwiches, and wimpy-diddles.

ANNIVERSARY CELEBRATED
Mr. and Mrs. Alfred Toodle celebrated their 70th wedding anniversary at a dinner given by seven of their 11 children: Richard Toodle, Emil Toodle, Joseph Toodle, Conrad Toodle, Donna Toodle, Dorothy (Toodle) Fugtree, and Estelle (Toodle) Campbell. Also present were 30 grandchildren, 82 great-grandchildren, and 13 great-great-grandchildren. The dinner was held at the Toodle Family Restaurant. The sheet cake was decorated by Betsy Ann Toodle.

During the uproar (everyone was reading aloud) the Press Club manager sidled up to the head table and whispered in the host's ear. "Long distance for you, Qwill. In my office."

Before hurrying to the phone, Qwilleran shouted, "Thanks for coming, everyone! The bar's open!"

He was absent from the dining room long enough to make a few phone calls of his own, and when he returned he dragged Junior away from a group of editors and reporters.

"We've gotta get out, Junior. We're going home. I've changed our reservations. . . . Arch, tell everyone goodbye for us, will you? It's an emergency. . . . Come on, Junior."

"What? . . . What?" Junior spluttered.

"Tell you later."

"My sack—"

"Forget your sack."

Qwilleran hustled the young man down the steps of the club and pushed him into the cab that waited at the curb with motor running.

"Hotel Stilton on the double," he yelled to the driver as the cab shot forward, "and run the red lights."

"Oh, wow!" Junior said.

"How fast can you throw your things in your duffel, kid? We've got seven minutes to pack, check out, and get up to the heliport on the hotel roof."

Not until they had piled into the police helicopter did Qwilleran take time to explain. "Urgent phone call from Pickax," he shouted. "The Big One is moving in. Gotta beat it—personal emergency. Get ready to run. They're holding the plane."

When they finally buckled up on the jet, Junior said, "Hey, how did you swing that deal? I've never been on a chopper."

"It helps if you've worked at the *Fluxion*," Qwilleran explained, "and if you've cooperated with Homicide and plugged the Police Widows' Fund. Sorry to spoil the rest of our plans."

"That's okay. I don't mind missing the other stuff."

"We can make a fast connection in Chicago and

then catch the TGIF commuter out of Minneapolis. We're lucky it worked out that way."

For the rest of the flight Qwilleran was reluctant to talk, but Junior couldn't stop. "Everybody was great! The sportswriters said they'd get me into the press box any time I'm in town. . . . The guy that runs the 'Newsroom Mouse' column is going to write up the *Picayune* on Tuesday, and that's syndicated all over the country, you know. How about that? . . . Mr. Bates said I could have a job any time I want to leave Pickax."

Qwilleran reserved comment. He was familiar with the managing editor's promises; the man had a short memory.

Junior chattered on. "They hire a lot of women at the *Fluxion*, don't they? On the desk, general assignment, heads of departments, photographers. Do you know that redheaded photographer—the one with green stockings?"

Qwilleran shook his head. "She's new since I left the paper."

"She's a photojournalist, and she free-lances for national magazines. She might come up to Moose County next spring and do a picture story on the abandoned mines. Not bad!"

"Not bad," Qwilleran echoed quietly.

He was still abnormally quiet when they boarded the tiny commuter after midnight. He occupied the window seat, and when he turned to listen to Junior he could see a man sitting across the aisle, holding an open magazine. The passenger stared at the same page throughout the flight.

He isn't reading, Qwilleran thought. He's listening. And he doesn't belong up here. No one in Moose County has that buttoned-down cool.

At the airport terminal the stranger went to the counter to rent a car.

"Junior," Qwilleran muttered, "who's the guy in the black raincoat?"

"Never saw him before," Junior said. "Looks like a traveling salesman."

The man was no traveling salesman, Qwilleran told himself. There was something about his walk, his manner, the way he appraised his surroundings . . .

As they drove back to Pickax in the early hours of the morning, Junior finally showed signs of running out of exuberance, and he noticed Qwilleran's preoccupied silence. "Anything wrong at your house, Qwill? You said it was an emergency."

"It's an emergency, but not at my house. Your mother called my housekeeper, and Mrs. Cobb phoned the Press Club. You're needed at home in a hurry. There's no storm moving in; I lied to you about that." Qwilleran made a right turn at the traffic light.

"Hey! Where are you going? Aren't you dropping me at the farm?"

"We're going to the hospital. There's been an accident. A car accident."

"*My dad?*" Junior shouted. "How serious?"

"Very bad. Your mother's waiting for you at the hospital. I don't know how to say this, Junior, but I've got to tell you. Your dad was killed instantly. It was on the bridge—the old plank bridge."

They pulled up at the side door of the hospital. Junior jumped out of the car without a word and bolted into the building.

TWO

Monday, November eleventh. "Heavy cloud cover throughout the county, with promise of snow before nightfall. Present temperature in Pickax, twenty-two degrees, with a windchill factor of ten below."—So said the WPKX meteorologist.

On Monday morning the schools, stores, offices, and restaurants of Pickax were closed until noon—for the funeral. The day was cold, gray, damp, and miserable. Yet, crowds milled about the Old Stone Church on Park Circle. Other onlookers huddled in the little circular park—shivering, stamping feet, swinging arms, clapping mittened hands together, anything to keep warm, and that included a furtive swig from a half-pint bottle in desperate cases. They were expecting to see a record broken: the longest funeral procession since 1904.

Police cars blockaded downtown Main Street to facilitate the formation of the procession. Cars bearing purple flags on the fender were lined up four abreast from curb to curb.

Qwilleran, moving through the crowd in the park, watched faces and listened to the low, respectful hum of voices. Small boys who climbed on the fountain for a better view were shooed away by a police officer and admonished if they shrieked or raced through the crowd.

Gathered inside the church were the numerous branches of the Goodwinter clan, as well as city officials, members of the Chamber of Commerce, and the country club set. Outside the church were the readers of the *Picayune*: businessmen, housewives, farmers, retirees, waitresses, laborers, hunters. They were witnessing an event they would remember all their lives and describe to future generations, just as their grandparents had described the funeral of Ephraim Goodwinter.

Among them was one man who was obviously foreign to the scene. He wandered through the crowd, glancing alertly in all directions, studying faces. He was wearing a black raincoat, and Qwilleran hoped it had a heavy lining; the cold was bone chilling.

A hunter in orange-and-black camouflage was

mumbling to a man who wore a feed cap and had a cheek full of snuff. "Gonna be a long one. Longer than Captain Fugtree's, looks like."

The farmer shifted his chew. "Near a hundred, I reckon. The captain had seventy-five, they said in the paper."

"Lucky they could bury him before snow flies. There's a Big One headed this way, they said on radio."

"Can't believe nothin' they say on radio. That storm from Canada blowed itself out afore it got anywheres near the border."

"Where'd it happen?" the hunter asked. "The accident, I mean."

"Old plank bride. It's a bugger! We been after the county to get off their duff and widen the danged thing. They say he rammed the stone rail, flipped head over tail, landed on the rocks in the river. Car caught fire. It's a closed casket, I hear."

"They should sue somebody."

"Prob'ly goin' too fast. Mebbe hit a deer."

"Or coulda been he was on a Friday night toot," the hunter said with a sly grin.

"Not him! *She's* the one that's the barfly. With him it was never nothin' but work work work. Fell asleep at the wheel, betcha. Whole family's jinxed. Y'know what happened to his old man."

"Yeah, but he prob'ly deserved it, from what I hear."

"And then there was his uncle. Somethin' fishy about *that* story!"

"And his grandfather. They never got the low-down on what happened to him. What'll they do with the paper now?"

"The kid'll take over," the farmer said. "Fourth generation. No tellin' what he'll take it into his head to do. These young ones go away to school and get some loony ideas."

Voices hushed as the bell began to toll a single solemn note and the casket was carried from the church, followed by the bereaved family. The heavily veiled widow was accompanied by her elder son. Junior walked with his sister from Montana. On the sidewalk and in the park the townspeople crossed themselves and men removed their headgear. There was a long wait as the mourners moved silently to their cars, directed by young men in black car coats and ambassador hats of black fur. At a signal, men in uniform fell into rank and hoisted brass instruments. Then, with the Pickax Funeral Band playing a doleful march, the long line of cars started to move forward.

Qwilleran pulled down the earflaps of his winter hat, turned up his coat collar, and headed across the park to the place he now called home.

The Klingenschoen residence that Qwilleran had inherited was one of five important buildings on the Park Circle, where Main Street divided and circumvented a little grassy plot with stone benches and a stone fountain. On one side of the circle were the Old Stone Church, the Little Stone Church, and a venerable courthouse. Facing them across the park were the public library and the K mansion, as Pickax natives called it. A massive cube of fieldstone three stories high, the mansion occupied its spacious grounds with the regal assurance that it was the most impressive edifice in town, and the costliest.

For a man who had chosen to spend his adult life in apartments and hotels, always on the move like a gypsy, the palatial residence was a discomfort, an embarrassment. Eventually Qwilleran would deed it to the city as a museum, but for five years he was doomed to live with the Klingenschoen brand of conspicuous consumption: vast rooms with four-teen-foot ceilings and ornate woodwork; crystal chandeliers by the ton and Oriental rugs by the acre; priceless French and English antiques, and art objects worth millions.

Qwilleran solved his problem by moving into the old servants' quarters above the garage, while the housekeeper occupied a sumptuous French suite in the main house.

Housekeeper was a misnomer for Iris Cobb. A former antique dealer and appraiser from Down Below, she now functioned as house manager, registrar of the collection, and curator of an architectural masterpiece destined to become a museum. She was also an obsessive cook who liked to putter about the kitchen—a dumpy figure in a faded pink smock. Despite her career credentials the widowed Mrs. Cobb baked endless cookies and pies with which to please the opposite sex, and she was inclined to gaze at men worshipfully through her thick-lensed eye-glasses.

Mrs. Cobb had a hearty oyster stew waiting for Qwilleran when he returned from the funeral. "I looked out the window and saw all the cars," she said. "The procession must be half a mile long!"

"Longest in Pickax history," Qwilleran said. "It's not only the funeral of a man; it may turn out to be the funeral of a century-old newspaper."

"Did you see the widow? She must be taking it terribly hard." Mrs. Cobb related emotionally to any woman who lost a husband, having experienced two such tragedies herself.

"Mrs. Goodwinter's three grown children were with her—also an older woman, probably Junior's Grandma Gage. She was tiny, but as straight as a brigadier general. . . . Any phone calls while I was out, Mrs. Cobb?"

"No, but a busboy from the Old Stone Mill brought over some pork liver cupcakes. It's a new idea, and the chef would like your opinion. I put them in the freezer."

Qwilleran grunted in disgust. "I'll give that clown an opinion—fast! I wouldn't touch a pork liver cupcake if he paid me!"

"Oh, they're not people food, Mr. Q! They're for the cats. The chef is experimenting with a line of frozen gourmet dinners for pets."

"Well, take a couple out of the freezer, and the spoiled brats can have them for supper. By the way, have you noticed any books on the floor in the library? Koko is pushing them off the shelf, and I don't approve of his new hobby."

"I tidied up this morning and didn't notice anything."

"He's particularly attracted to those small volumes of Shakespeare in pigskin bindings. Yesterday I found *Hamlet* on the floor."

Behind Mrs. Cobb's thick lenses there was a mischievous twinkle. "Do you think he knows I've got a baked ham in the fridge?"

"He has devious ways of communicating, Mrs. Cobb, but that would be a new low," Qwilleran said. "What is today? Monday? I suppose you're going out tonight. If so, I'll feed the cats."

The housekeeper's face brightened. "Herb Hackpole is taking me out to dinner—somewhere special, he said. I hope it's the Old Stone Mill. They say the food's wonderful since the new chef took over."

Qwilleran huffed into his moustache, a private sign of disapproval. "It's about time that skinflint took you out to dinner! It seems to me you always go over to his place and cook for him."

"But I like to!" Mrs. Cobb said, with her eyes shining.

Hackpole was a used-car dealer with a reputation for being obnoxious, but she found him attractive. The man had red devils tattooed on his arms and wore his thinning hair in a crew cut, and he often neglected to shave, but she liked men in the rough. Qwilleran recalled that her late husband had been an uncouth lout and she loved him deeply. Now, since starting to date Hackpole, her round cheerful face had become positively radiant.

"If you want to have someone in for dinner," Mrs. Cobb said, "you can serve the baked ham, and I'll make the ginger-pear salad you like, and I'll put a sweet potato casserole in the oven. All you have to do is take it out when the bell rings." She was acquainted with Qwilleran's helplessness in the kitchen.

"That's very thoughtful of you," he said. "I might invite Mrs. Duncan."

"Oh, that would be nice!" The housekeeper's expression was conspiratorial, as if she sensed a romance. "I'll set the marquetry table in the library with a Madeira cloth and candles and everything. It will be nice and cozy for two. Mr. O'Dell can lay a fire with those applewood logs. They smell so good!"

"Don't make it too obviously seductive," Qwilleran requested. "The lady is rather proper."

"She's a lovely person, Mr. Q, and just the right age for you, if you don't mind me saying so. She has a lot of personality for a librarian."

"It's a new trend," he said. "Libraries now have fewer books but a lot of audiovisuals . . . and champagne parties . . . and personality all over the place."

After lunch Qwilleran walked around the Park Circle to the public library, which masqueraded as a Greek temple. It had been built by the founder of the *Picayune* at the turn of the century, and a portrait of Ephraim Goodwinter hung in the lobby, although it was partly obscured by a display of new video materials and there was a slash in the canvas that had been poorly repaired.

The after-school crowd had not yet swarmed into the library with homework assignments, so four friendly young clerks rushed to Qwilleran's assistance. Young women were always attracted to the man with a luxuriant moustache and mournful eyes. Furthermore, he served on the library's board of trustees. Furthermore, he was the richest man in town.

He asked the clerks a simple question, and they all dashed away at once in several directions—one to the card catalogue, one to the local-history shelf, and two to the computer. The answer from all sources was negative. He thanked them and headed for the chief librarian's office on the balcony.

Carrying his lumberjack mackinaw and woodsman's hat, Qwilleran bounded up the stairs three at a time, thinking pleasant thoughts. Polly Duncan was a charming though enigmatic woman, and she had a speaking voice that he found both soothing and stimulating.

She looked up from her desk and gave him a cordial but businesslike smile. "What a pleasant surprise, Qwill! What urgent mission brings you up here in such a hurry?"

"I came chiefly to hear your mellifluous voice," he said, turning on a little charm himself. And then he quoted one of his favorite lines from Shakespeare. *"Her voice was ever soft, gentle and low—an excellent thing in woman."*

"That's from *King Lear*, act five, scene three," she replied promptly.

"Polly, your memory is incredible!" he said. *"I am amazed and know not what to say."*

"That's Hermia's line in act three, scene two, of *A Midsummer Night's Dream*. . . . Don't look so surprised, Qwill. I told you my father was a Shakespeare scholar. We children knew the plays as well as our peers knew the big-league batting averages. . . . Did you go to the funeral this morning?"

"I observed from the park, and it gave me an idea. According to the phalanx of eager assistants downstairs, no one has ever written a history of the *Picayune*. I'd like to try it. How much is there to work with?"

"Let me think. . . . You could start with the Goodwinters in our genealogical collection."

"Do you have back copies of the newspaper?"

"Only for the last twenty years. Prior to that, everything was destroyed by mice or burst steam pipes or mismanagement. But I'm sure the *Picayune* office has a complete file."

"Is there anyone I could interview? Anyone who would remember back sixty or seventy-five years?"

"You might check with the Old Timers Club. They're all over eighty. Euphonia Gage is the president."

"Is that the woman who drives a Mercedes and blows the horn a lot?"

"A succinct description! Senior Goodwinter was her son-in-law, and since she has a reputation for brutal candor, she might supply some choice information."

"Polly, you're a gem! By the way, are you free for dinner tonight? Mrs. Cobb is preparing a repast that's too good for a lonely bachelor. I thought you might consent to share it."

"Delighted! I must not stay too late, but I hope there will be time for reading aloud after dinner. You have a marvelous voice, Qwill."

"Thank you." He preened his moustache with pleasure. "I'll go home and gargle."

Turning to leave, he glanced across the balcony to the reading room. "Who's that man over there—with a pile of books on the table?"

"A historian from Down Below, doing research on early mining operations. He asked if I could recommend any good restaurants, and I suggested Stephanie's and the Old Stone Mill. Do you have any other ideas?"

"I think I do," said Qwilleran. He clapped his hat on his head at a wild angle and clomped around the balcony in his yellow duck boots, stopping at the table where the stranger was seated.

In a parody of a friendly north-country native he said, "Howdy! Lady over yonder says yer lookin' fer a place to chow down. Fer a real good feed y'oughta try Otto's Tasty Eats. All y'can eat fer fi' bucks. How long y'gonna be aroun'?"

"Until I finish my work," the historian said crisply, bending over his book.

"If y'wanna shot-na-beer y'oughta try the Hotel Booze. Good burgers, too."

"Thank you," the man said in a tone of dismissal.

"I see y'be readin' 'bout them ol' mines. M'grampaw got killed in a cave-in back in 1913. I weren't born yit. Seen any ol' mines?"

"No," the man said, snapping his book shut and pushing his chair back.

"Nearest hereabouts be the Dimsdale. They got a diner there. Good place t'git a plate o' beans 'n' franks."

Clutching his black raincoat, the stranger walked rapidly to the stairway.

Pleased with the man's exasperation and his own performance, Qwilleran straightened his hat, bundled up in his mackinaw, and went on his way. He knew by the man's obvious lack of interest that he was not what he claimed to be.

At 5:30 Herb Hackpole arrived to pick up his dinner partner, parking in the side drive and tooting the horn. Mrs. Cobb scurried out the back door as excited as a young girl on her first date.

At 5:45 Qwilleran fed the cats. Pork liver cupcakes, when thawed, became a revolting gray mush, but the Siamese crouched over the plate and devoured the chef's innovation with tails flat on the floor, denoting total satisfaction.

At 6:00 Polly Duncan arrived—on foot—having left her small six-year-old maroon car behind the library. If it were seen in the circular driveway of the K mansion, the gossips of Pickax would have a field day. Everyone knew what everyone else drove—make, model, year, and color.

Polly was not as young and slender as the career women he had dated Down Below, but she was an interesting woman with a voice that sometimes made his head spin, and she looked like a comfortable armful, although he had not tested his theory. The librarian maintained a certain reserve, despite her show of friendliness, and she always insisted on going home early.

He greeted her at the front door, a masterpiece of carving and polished brass. "Where's the snow they promised?" he asked.

"Every day in November WPKX predicts snow as a matter of policy," she said, "and sooner or later they're right. . . . This house never fails to overwhelm me!"

She was gazing in wonder at the foyer's amber leather walls and grand staircase, extravagantly wide and elaborately balustered. The dazzling chandelier was Baccarat crystal. The rugs were Anatolian antiques. "This house doesn't belong in Pickax; it belongs in Paris. It amazes me that the Klingenschoens owned such treasures and no one knew about it."

"It was the Klingenschoens' revenge—for not being accepted socially." Qwilleran escorted her to the rear of the house. "We're having dinner in the library, but Mrs. Cobb wants me to show you her mobile herb garden in the solarium."

The stone-floored room had large glass areas, a forest of ancient rubber plants, and some wicker chairs for summer lounging; the winter addition was a wrought-iron cart with eight clay pots labeled mint, dill, thyme, basil, and the like.

"It can be wheeled around during the day to get the best sunlight," he explained. "That is—if WPKX allows us to have any."

Polly nodded approval. "Herbs like sun but not too much heat. Where did Mrs. Cobb find this clever contraption?"

"She designed it, and a friend of hers made it in his welding shop. Perhaps you know Hackpole, the used-car dealer."

"Yes, his garage has just winterized my car. How do you like your new front-wheel drive, Qwill?"

"I'll know better when snow flies."

In the library the lamps were lighted, logs were blazing in the fireplace, and the table was laid with a dazzling display of porcelain, crystal, and silver. The four walls of books were accented by marble busts of Homer, Dante, and Shakespeare.

"Did the Klingenschoens read these books?" Polly asked.

"I think they were primarily for show, except for a few racy novels from the 1920s. In the attic I found boxes of paperback mysteries and romances."

"At least someone was *reading*. There is still hope for the printed word." She handed him a book with worn and faded cover. "Here's something that might interest you—*Picturesque Pickax*, published by the Boosters Club before World War One. On the page with the bookmark there's a picture of the *Picayune* building with employees standing on the sidewalk."

Qwilleran found the photo of anxious-faced men with walrus moustaches, high collars, leather aprons, eyeshades, arm garters, and plastered hair parted in the middle. "They look as if they're facing a firing squad," he said. "Thanks. This will be useful."

He poured an aperitif for his guest. Dry sherry was her choice; one glass was her limit. For himself he poured white grape juice.

"*Votre santé!*" he toasted, meeting her eyes.

"*Santé!*" she replied with a guarded gaze.

She was wearing the somber gray suit, white blouse, and maroon loafers that seemed to be her library uniform, but she had tried to perk it up with a paisley scarf. Fashion was not one of her pursuits, and her severe haircut was not in the latest style, but her voice. . . ! It was ever soft, gentle, and low, and she knew Shakespeare forward and backward.

After a moment of silence during which Qwilleran wondered what Polly was thinking, he said, "Do you remember that so-called historian in your reading room? He had a pile of books on old mining operations. I doubt that he's telling the truth."

"Why do you say that?"

"His relaxed posture. The way he held his book. He didn't show a researcher's avid thirst for information, and he wasn't taking notes. He was reading idly to kill time."

"Then who is he? Why should he disguise his identity?"

"I think he's an investigator. Narcotics—FBI— something like that."

Polly looked skeptical. "In Pickax?"

"I'm sure there are several skeletons in local closets, Polly, and most of the locals know all about them. You have some world-class gossips here."

"I wouldn't call them gossips," she said defensively. "In small towns people *share information*. It's a way of *caring*."

Qwilleran raised a cynical eyebrow. "Well, the mysterious stranger had better complete his mission before snow flies, or he'll be cluttering up your reading room until spring thaw. . . . Another question. What will happen to the *Picayune* now that Senior's gone? Any guesses?"

"It will probably die a quiet death—an idea that has outlived its time."

"How well have you known Junior's parents?"

"Only casually. Senior was a workaholic—an agreeable man, but not at all social. Gritty likes the country club life—golf, cards, dinner dances. I wanted her to serve on my board of trustees, but it was too dull for her taste."

"Gritty? Is that Mrs. Goodwinter's name?"

"Gertrude, actually, but there's a certain clique here that clings to their adolescent nicknames: Muffy, Buffy, Bunky, Dodo. I must admit that Mrs.

Goodwinter has an abundance of grit, for good or ill. She's like her mother. Euphonia Gage is a spunky woman."

A distant buzzer sounded, and Qwilleran lighted the candles, dropped a Fauré cassette in the player, and served dinner.

"You obviously know everyone in Pickax," he remarked.

"For a newcomer I don't do badly. I've been here only . . . twenty-five years."

"I had a hunch you were from the East. New England?"

She nodded. "While I was in college I married a native of Pickax, and we came here to manage his family's bookstore. Unfortunately it closed soon after—when my husband was killed—but I didn't want to go back east."

"He must have been very young."

"Very young. He was a volunteer fire fighter. I remember one dry windy day in August. Our bookstore was a block from the fire hall, and when the siren sounded, my husband dashed from the store. Traffic stopped dead, and men came running from all directions—running hard, pounding the pavement, pumping their arms. The mechanic from the gas station, one of the young pastors, a bartender, the hardware man—all running as if their lives depended on it. Then cars and trucks with revolving lights pulled up and parked anywhere, and the drivers jumped out and ran to the fire hall. By that time the big doors were open, and the tanker and pumper were moving out, with men clinging to the trucks and putting on their gear."

"You describe it vividly, Polly."

Tears came to her eyes. "It was a barn fire, and he was killed by a falling timber."

There was a long silence.

"That's a sad story," Qwilleran said.

"The fire fighters were so conscientious. When the siren sounded, they dropped everything and ran. In the middle of the night they'd wake from a sound sleep, pull on some clothes, and run. Yet they were criticized: arrived too late . . . not enough men . . . didn't pump enough water . . . equipment broke down." She sighed. "They tried so hard. They still do. They're all volunteers, you know."

"Junior Goodwinter is a volunteer," Qwilleran said, "and his beeper is always sounding off in the middle of something. . . . What did you do after that windy day in August?"

"I went to work at the library and found contentment here."

"Pickax has a human scale that is—what shall I say?—comforting. Tranquilizing. But why are we all obsessed with the weather reports?"

"We're close to the elements," Polly said. "The weather affects everything: farming, lumbering, commercial fishing, outdoor sports. And we all drive long distances over country roads. There are no taxis we can call on a bad day."

Mrs. Cobb had left the coffee maker plugged in

and pots of chocolate mousse in the refrigerator, and the meal ended pleasantly.

"Where are the cats?" Polly asked.

"Shut up in the kitchen. Koko has been pulling books off the shelf. He thinks he's a librarian. Yum Yum, on the other hand, is just a cat who chases her tail and steals paper clips and hides things under the rug. Every time my foot comes down on a bump in the rug, I wince. Is it my wristwatch? Or a mouse? Or my reading glasses? Or a crumpled envelope from the wastebasket?"

"What titles has Koko recommended?"

"He's on a Shakespeare kick," Qwilleran said. "It may have something to do with the pigskin bindings. Just before you arrived, he pushed *A Midsummer Night's Dream* off the shelf."

"That's a coincidence," Polly said. "I'm named after one of the characters." She paused and waited for him to guess.

"Hippolyta?"

"Correct! My father named all of us after characters in the plays. My brothers are Marc Antony and Brutus, and my poor sister Ophelia has had to endure bawdy remarks ever since the fifth grade. . . . Why don't you let the cats out? I'd like to see Koko in action."

When they were released, Yum Yum walked daintily into the library, placing one paw in front of the other and looking for a vacant lap, but Koko flaunted his independence by delaying his entrance. It was not until Qwilleran and his guest heard a *thunk* that they realized Koko was in the room. On the floor lay the thin volume of *King Henry VIII*.

Qwilleran said, "You have to admit he knows what he's doing. There's a gripping scene for a woman in the play—where the queen confronts the two cardinals."

"It's tremendous!" Polly said. "Katherine claims to be a poor weak woman but she blasts the two learned men. *'Ye have angels' faces, but heaven knows your hearts!'* Do you ever wonder about the true identity of Shakespeare, Qwill?"

"I've read that the plays may have been written by Jonson or Oxford."

"I think Shakespeare was a woman. There are so many strong female roles and wonderful speeches for women."

"And there are strong male roles and wonderful speeches for men," he replied.

"Yes, but I contend that a woman can write strong male roles more successfully than a man can write good women's roles."

"Hmmm," said Qwilleran politely.

Koko was now sitting tall on the desk, obviously waiting for something, and Qwilleran obliged by reading the prologue of the play. Then Polly gave a stirring reading of the queen's confrontation scene.

"Yow!" said Koko.

"Now I must go," she said, "before my landlord starts to worry."

"Your landlord?"

"Mr. MacGregor is a nice old widower," she explained. "I rent a cottage on his farm, and he thinks women shouldn't go out alone at night. He sits up waiting for me to drive in."

"Have you ever tried your Shakespeare theory on your landlord?" Qwilleran asked.

After Polly had said a gracious thank-you and a brisk good-night, Qwilleran questioned her excuse for leaving early. At least Koko had not ordered her out of the house, as he had done other female visitors in the past. That was a good sign.

Qwilleran was removing the dinner dishes and tidying the kitchen when Mrs. Cobb returned from her date, flushed and happy.

"Oh, you don't need to do that, Mr. Q," she said.

"No trouble at all. Thank you for a superb meal. How was your evening?"

"We went to the Old Stone Mill. The food is much better now. I had a gorgeous stuffed trout with wine sauce. Herb ordered steak Diane, but he didn't like the sauce."

That guy, Qwilleran thought, would prefer ketchup. To Mrs. Cobb he said, "Mrs. Duncan was telling me about the volunteer fire department. Isn't Hackpole a fireman?"

"Yes, and he's had some thrilling experiences—carrying children from a burning building, reviving people with CPR, herding cows from a burning barn!"

Interesting if true, Qwilleran thought. "Bring him in for a nightcap next time you go out," he suggested. "I'd like to know how a small-town fire department operates."

"Oh, thank you, Mr. Q! He'll be pleased. He thinks you don't like him, because you took him to court once."

"Nothing personal. I simply objected to being attacked by a dog that should be chained according to law. If you like him, Mrs. Cobb, I'm sure he's a good man."

As Qwilleran was locking up for the night, the telephone rang. It was Junior Goodwinter's voice, crackling with excitement. "She's coming! She's flying up here tomorrow!"

"Who's coming?"

"The photojournalist I met at the Press Club. She says the *Fluxion* is running the column tomorrow, and it'll be all over the country this week. She wants to submit a picture story to a news magazine while it's hot."

"Did you tell her . . . about your father?"

"She says that will only make it topical. I have to pick her up at the airport tomorrow morning. We're going to get some Old Timers who used to work at the *Pic* to pose in the shots. Do you realize what this could do? It'll put Pickax on the map! And it could put the *Picayune* back in business if we start getting subscriptions from all over."

Stranger things have happened, Qwilleran thought. "Call me tomorrow night after the shoot. Let me know how it goes. And good luck!"

As he replaced the telephone receiver he heard a

soft sound, *thlunk*, as another book landed on the Bokhara rug. Koko was sitting on the Shakespeare shelf, looking proud of himself.

Qwilleran picked up the book and smoothed the crumpled pages. It was *Hamlet* again, and a line in the first scene caught his eye: " *'Tis now struck twelve; get thee to bed.*"

Addressing the cat he said, "You may think you're smart, but this has got to stop! These books are printed on fine India paper. They can't stand this kind of treatment."

"Ik ik ik," said Koko, following his remark with a yawn.

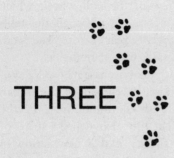

THREE

Tuesday, November twelfth. "Snow flurries during the day, then falling temperatures and winds shifting to northeast." So said WPKX, and Mr. O'Dell, the houseman, waxed his snow shovels and checked the spark plugs on his snowblower.

It was the day after the pork liver cupcakes had made their successful debut, and Qwilleran planned to lunch at the Old Stone Mill—to report results to the chef, and to solve a mystery that had been bothering him.

Who was this chef?

What was his name?

Where did he come from?

What were his credentials?

And why had no one seen him?

The restaurant was an old gristmill with a giant waterwheel, recently renovated with good taste. The stone walls and massive timbers were exposed; the maple floor was sanded to the color of honey; and every table had a view of the mill wheel, which creaked and turned incessantly although the mill-stream had dried up seventy years before. The food, everyone had always said, was abominable.

Then the restaurant was purchased by XYZ Enterprises, Inc., of Pickax, developers of the Indian Village apartments and condominiums on the Ittibittiwassee River. The firm also owned a string of party stores in the county and a new motel in Mooseville.

One day at a Chamber of Commerce meeting Qwilleran was approached by Don Exbridge, the X of XYZ Enterprises. He was a string bean of a man, six-feet-five, with a smile that had made him popular and successful.

"Qwill, you have restaurant connections Down Below," said Exbridge. "Where can we get a good chef for the Old Stone Mill? Preferably someone who enjoys the outdoors and doesn't mind living in the boonies."

"I'll give it some thought and get back to you," Qwilleran had promised.

Then the wheels started turning in his mind: Hixie Rice, former neighbor Down Below . . . member of a select gourmet group . . . loved to eat, and her figure proved it . . . clever young woman . . . unlucky in love . . . worked in advertising and promotion . . . used to speak French to Koko. Why, Qwilleran wondered, were all the clever ones in advertising while all the hardworking serious thinkers were in journalism, earning less money?

The last time he had heard from Hixie, she was dating a chef and was taking courses in restaurant management. And that was how Hixie Rice and her chef happened to land in Pickax. Immediately they replaced the dreary menu with more sophisticated dishes and fresh ingredients. The chef retrained the existing kitchen staff, locked up the deep fryers, and rationed the salt.

When Qwilleran went to lunch at the Old Stone Mill on Tuesday, he hardly recognized the former member of the Friendly Fatties. "Hixie, you're looking almost anorexic!" he said. "Have you stopped putting butter on your bacon and sugar on your hot fudge sundae?"

"You won't believe it, Qwill, but the restaurant business has cured my obsession for eating," she said. "All that *food* turns me off. Fifteen pounds of butter . . . a two-foot wheel of cheese . . . two hundred chickens . . . thirty dozen eggs! Have you ever seen two hundred *naked chickens*, Qwill?"

In losing weight, Hixie had also lost her wheezy high-pitched voice, and her hair now looked healthy and natural instead of contrived and varnished. "You're looking great!" he told her.

"And you look *super*, Qwill. Your voice sounds different."

"I've stopped smoking. Rosemary convinced me to give up my pipe."

"Do you still see Rosemary?"

"No, she's living in Toronto."

"All our old gourmet gang is scattered, but I thought you two were headed for holy bondage."

"There was a personality clash between Rosemary and Koko," he explained.

Hixie seated him near the turning mill wheel. "This is considered a choice table," she said, "although the motion of the wheel makes some of our customers seasick. It's the *creaking* that drives me up the wall, and the tape recording of a rushing millstream has a psychological effect on diners. They're wearing out the carpet to the rest room." She handed him a menu. "The lamb shank with ratatouille is good today."

"How about the fresh salmon?"

"It's off the blackboard. You're a little late."

"It was premeditated," Qwilleran said. "I'd like to talk with you. Can you join me?"

He ordered the lamb, and Hixie sat down with a glass of Campari and a cigarette. "How did Koko and Yum Yum like the cupcakes?" she asked.

"After they ate the things they chased each other up and down stairs for two hours, and they're both neutered! Have you discovered a feline aphrodisiac?"

"That's only the first of several frozen catfoods

we want to market. The XYZ people are backing us financially. Fabulous Frozen Foods for Fussy Felines! How does that sound?"

"When are you and your partner going to come over and speak French to Koko? You haven't seen the magnificent dump I live in."

"It's difficult to socialize," she apologized. "We work such *rotten* hours. They never told me about that in restaurant school. I'm not complaining; in fact, I'm *deliriously* happy! I used to be a loser, you know, but all that has changed since I've found a wonderful man. He's not a drunk; he doesn't do drugs; and he's not some other woman's husband."

"I'm very happy for you," Qwilleran said. "When am I going to meet the guy?"

"He's not here right now."

"What's his name? What does he look like?"

"Tony Peters, and he's tall, blond, and *very* good-looking."

"Where did he learn to cook?"

"Montreal . . . Paris . . . other good places."

"I'd like to meet the guy and shake his hand. After all, I'm responsible for bringing you both to this northern paradise."

"*Actually,*" Hixie said, "he's out of town. His mother had a stroke, and he had to fly to Philadelphia."

"He'd better get back before snow flies, or he'll have to make the trip on snowshoes. The airport closes down after the Big One. Where are you living?"

"We have a *super* apartment in Indian Village. Mr. Exbridge pulled strings to get us in. There's a waiting list, you know."

"And what do you do on your day off?"

"Tony's writing a cookbook. I check out the competition around the county."

"Have you made any interesting discoveries?"

"Next to the Old Stone Mill, Stephanie's has the best food," Hixie said, "but their chef has some kind of mental *block*. I ordered a stuffed artichoke and got a stuffed *avocado*. When the waiter insisted it was an artichoke, I grabbed my plate and stormed out to the kitchen to confront the chef, and that arrogant *clod* had the nerve to tell me I didn't know a stuffed artichoke from a stuffed crocodile! I was furious! I informed him that an artichoke is a member of the thistle family, and an avocado is a pear-shaped fruit that gets its name from the Nahuatl word for testicle, although I assume he wouldn't know anything about *that*!"

"How did he react?"

"He picked up a cleaver and started flattening chicken breasts, so I retreated before I became a homicide statistic."

Later that afternoon Qwilleran sat at his desk in the library and wondered about Hixie and her mysterious companion. Koko jumped to the desktop, sat tall, and cocked his head expectantly.

"Do you remember Hixie?" Qwilleran asked him. "She was taking French lessons and used to say,

'*Bonjour, Monsieur Koko.*' She always got involved with marginal types of men, and now she has this invisible chef. There's something strange about him, and yet his kitchen is turning out great food. I brought you a chunk of lamb shank in a doggie bag. Hixie was glad you liked the cupcakes."

Koko wriggled his posterior, squeezed his eyes, and murmured a falsetto "Ik ik."

At that moment Mrs. Cobb peered inquiringly into the room.

"I heard you talking and thought you had company, Mr. Q. I was going to suggest some tea and cookies. I've just baked butterscotch pecan meringues."

"I'm only having an intelligent dialogue with Koko, as Lori Bamba recommended," he explained. "I feel like an idiot, but he seems to enjoy it. By the way, I'll accept some of those butterscotch things, but make it coffee instead of tea."

She bustled off to the kitchen, and Qwilleran went on. "Well, Koko, today was the big shoot at the *Picayune* office. For Junior's sake I hope something good comes of it. I wonder if the Old Timers held together long enough for the picture taking. They probably had to prop them up with two-by-fours and baling wire."

The day passed without the snow flurries predicted on the radio, but the temperature was dropping rapidly. Qwilleran was listening to the late-evening weathercast when Junior finally telephoned. His voice had none of the excitement of the previous day. He spoke in a minor key. Qwilleran thought, Something went wrong; the redhead failed to show; she decided it was no-story; she forgot her camera; her plane crashed; the Old Timers had heart attacks.

"Have you heard any rumors?" Junior was saying.

"About what?"

"About anything."

"I don't know what you're talking about, kid. Are you sober?"

"I wish I weren't," Junior said glumly. "Mind if I come over to see you? I know it's late . . ."

"Sure, come along."

"I'm at Jody's place. Okay if I bring her, too?"

"Of course. What do you two want to drink?"

"Make it coffee," Junior said after a moment's hesitation. "If I drink when I'm down, I'm liable to cut my wrists."

Qwilleran filled a thermal server with instant coffee and had a tray waiting in the library when the red Jaguar pulled into the drive.

Tiny Jody, with her straight blond hair and big blue eyes, looked like a china doll. Junior looked like an old man.

"Good God! What's happened to you?" Qwilleran said. "You look ghastly, Junior." He waved the young couple into the library.

Junior flopped on a leather sofa. "Bad news!"

"Didn't the shoot work out?"

"Oh sure, but a lot of good it will do. I feel like a fool, getting her to fly up here for nothing."

"You're talking in riddles, Junior. Let's have it!"

In her little-girl voice Jody said, "Tell Mr. Qwilleran about your mother, Juney."

The young newsman stared at Qwilleran for a silent moment before blurting out the news. "She's selling."

"Selling what?"

"Selling the *Picayune*."

Qwilleran frowned. "What is there to sell? There's nothing there but a . . . well . . . a quaint idea."

"That's the worst part," Junior said. "The *idea* and all those years of tradition are going down the drain. She's selling the *name*."

Qwilleran could neither believe nor comprehend. "Where does she expect to find a buyer?"

Jody piped up, "She's already got a buyer. XYZ Enterprises."

"They want to make it an advertising throwaway," said Junior, looking as if he might cry. "One of those free tabloids with junky ads and ink that comes off on your hands. No news matter. I tell you, Qwill, it's a kick in the gut."

"Has she a right to sell the paper? What about your father's will?"

"He left everything to her. All the assets are jointly held anyway—such as they are."

"Juney," said the small voice, "tell Mr. Qwilleran about your dream."

"Yeah, I've been dreaming about my father every night. He's just standing there in his leather apron and square paper hat, all covered with blood, and he's telling me something, but I can't hear it."

Qwilleran was trying to sort out his thoughts. "This has happened very fast, Junior. Your father was buried only yesterday. It's too quick a decision for a bereaved spouse to make. Have you suggested that to your mother?"

"What's the use? When she makes up her mind to do something, she does it."

"How do your brother and sister react?"

"My brother went back to California; he doesn't care. My sister thinks it's a crime, but she doesn't have any clout. Not with *our mother*! You've never met her."

"Was it her idea? Or did XYZ make an offer?"

Junior hesitated before answering. "Uh . . . I don't know."

"Why is she in such a hurry to sell?"

"Well, the money, you know. She needs money. Dad had a lot of debts, you know."

"Did he carry decent life insurance?"

"There's a policy, but it's not all that great. Grandma Gage has been keeping up the premiums for years, just to protect my mother and us. . . . The house is being sold, too."

"The farmhouse?"

"Isn't that sad?" Jody put in. "It's been in the Goodwinter family a hundred years."

Qwilleran said, "A widow should never make such a quick decision to change her lifestyle."

"Well, it's mortgaged, you know," Junior said,

"and she never wanted a big house anyway. She likes condominiums. She wants to unload the house before snow flies—doesn't want to be stuck with a big place in the country during the winter."

"That's understandable."

"She's going into an apartment in Indian Village."

"I thought there were no vacancies out there."

Jody said, "She's moving in with a *friend*," and Junior scowled at her.

"Can she find a buyer for the house that fast—without selling at a sacrifice?" Qwilleran asked.

"She's got a buyer."

"Who? Do you know who it is?"

"Herb Hackpole."

"Hackpole! What does a single man want with a big farmhouse like that?"

"Well, he's been wanting a place in the country, you know, so he can run his dogs. He has hunters. There's no acreage, but he'll be getting a good big yard and two barns."

"And what about the furnishings? You said your parents had a lot of family heirlooms."

"They're going to be auctioned off."

Jody said, "Juney had been promised his great-grandfather's desk, but that's going to be sold, too."

In a tone of defeat Junior said, "If they can squeeze in the auction before snow flies, they'll attract dealers from Ohio and Illinois and get the high dollar."

"And what about the antique printing presses in the barn?"

Junior shrugged. "They'll be sold for scrap metal. They figure the price by the ton."

The three of them fell into three kinds of silence: Junior, depressed; Jody, sympathetic; Qwilleran, stunned. Senior Goodwinter had been killed Friday night and buried Monday, and this was Tuesday.

"When did you hear about these drastic decisions, Junior?"

"My mother called me at the office this afternoon—right in the middle of the shoot. I didn't say anything to the photographer. Do you think I should have told her? It might kill the story—or take the edge off it. She left an hour ago. I drove her to the airport."

Suddenly Junior's beeper sounded. "Oh no!" he said. "That's all I need! A stupid barn fire! Take Jody home, will you, Qwill?" he called over his shoulder as he raced out of the house. The city hall siren was screaming. Police sirens were wailing.

It was then that Qwilleran realized he had forgotten to pour the coffee. "How about a cup, Jody? If it isn't too cold."

The tiny young woman curled up on the sofa, cradling the big mug in her small hands. "I feel so sorry for Juney. I told him to go Down Below and get a job at the *Daily Fluxion* and forget about everything up here."

"No one should act on impulse at a time like this," Qwilleran advised.

"Maybe he could get an injunction to stop her

from selling—or postpone it until she's thinking straight."

"Won't work. She'd have to be proved mentally incompetent. It's her own property now, and she can do whatever she wishes."

At that moment Mrs. Cobb, in robe and bedroom slippers, made an abrupt appearance in the doorway. "Look out the window!" she said in alarm. "There's a fire on Main Street! It looks like the lodge hall's on fire!"

Qwilleran and Jody jumped up, and all three of them hurried to the front windows.

"That's Herb's lodge," Mrs. Cobb said. "This is their meeting night. There could be thirty or forty people in the building."

"I'll drive down and see," Qwilleran said. "Come on, Jody, and I'll take you home afterward. Out this way . . . back door . . . car's in the garage."

Downtown Main Street was filled with flashing blue and red lights. Traffic was rerouted, and fire trucks were parked in an arc, training their headlights on the center of the block. The pumpers were working, and fire hoses were pouring water on the roof of the three-story lodge hall. Beyond that building there was an orange-red glow with flames leaping upward—then a hiss of steam—then a cloud of smoke.

Qwilleran parked, and he and Jody walked closer.

"It's the *Picayune*!" he shouted. "The whole building's on fire!"

Jody started to cry. "Poor Juney!" she kept saying. "Poor Juney!"

"They're hosing down the lodge hall to keep it from catching," Qwilleran said. "The post office, too. The newspaper plant is going to be totaled, I'm afraid."

"I think that's what his father was trying to tell him in the dream," she said. "Can you see Juney?"

"Can't recognize anyone in those helmets and rubber coats. Even their faces are black. Dirty job! The white helmet is the fire chief, that's all I can tell."

"I hope Juney doesn't do anything crazy, like running into the building to save something."

"They're trained not to take foolish risks," Qwilleran assured her.

"But he's so impulsive—and sentimental. That's why he's taking it so hard—his mother selling the *Pic*, I mean." A sudden look of horror crossed her face. "Oh, *no*! William Allen's in there! They always lock him up for the night. I'm going to be sick. . . ."

"Easy, Jody! He may have escaped. Cats are clever. . . . Come on. We can't stay here. It's icing up, and you're shivering. The men will be on the job for hours, mopping up and looking for hot spots. I'll drive you home. Will you be all right?"

"Yes, I'll wait up till Juney comes home. He's been staying at my place since his father died, you know."

At the K mansion Qwilleran found Mrs. Cobb at the kitchen table, still in her pink robe, drinking cocoa and looking worried. "There's no news on the radio," she said anxiously.

"It wasn't the lodge hall," Qwilleran told her. "It was the *Picayune* building. It's gutted. More than a century of publishing destroyed in half an hour."

"Did you see Herb?" She poured a cup of cocoa for Qwilleran. It was not his favorite beverage.

"No, but I'm sure he was there, swinging an ax."

"He shouldn't be doing such strenuous work. He's over fifty, you know, and most of the men are much younger."

"You seem unusually concerned about him, Mrs. Cobb." He gave her a searching look.

The housekeeper lowered her eyes and smiled sheepishly. "Well, I admit I'm fond of him. We always have a good time together, and he's beginning to drop hints."

"About *marriage*?" Qwilleran's dismay showed in his brusque question. As a housekeeper she was a jewel—too valuable to lose. She had spoiled him and the Siamese with her cooking.

"I wouldn't stop working, though," Mrs. Cobb hastened to say. "I've always worked, and this is the most wonderful job I ever had. It's a dream come true. I mean it!"

"And you're perfect for the position. Don't rush into anything, Mrs. Cobb."

"I won't," she promised. "He hasn't come right out and asked me yet, so don't you say anything."

She refilled her cocoa cup and carried it upstairs, saying a weary good-night.

Qwilleran made his nightly house check before setting the burglar alarm and locking up. Then he retired to his own quarters over the garage, carrying a wicker picnic hamper. Indistinct sounds came from inside the hamper, and it swung to and fro vigorously as he carried it.

The four-car garage was a former carriage house built of fieldstone—the same masonry that made the main house spectacular. There were four arched doors to the stalls, a cupola with a weather vane on the roof, and a brace of ornate carriage lanterns at each corner of the building.

Upstairs the interior had been refurbished to suit Qwilleran's taste—comfortable contemporary in soothing tones of beige, rust, and brown. It was quiet and simple, an escape from the pomp and preciosity of the K mansion.

In the sitting room there were easy chairs, good reading lamps, a music system, and a small bar where Qwilleran mixed drinks for guests. He himself had not touched alcohol since the time he fell off a subway platform in New York, an experience that had been permanently sobering. Nor had he ever ridden the subway again.

The other rooms were his writing studio, his bedroom, and the cats' parlor, which was carpeted and furnished with cushions, baskets, scratching posts, climbing trees, and a turkey roaster that served as their commode. There was also a shelf of secondhand books bought at the hospital bazaar for a dime apiece. There were books on first-year algebra and English grammar simplified. There was a collection of famous sermons. Other titles were *The Burning of Rome* and *Elsie Dinsmore* and Vergil's *Aeneid*. Koko could push them off the shelf to his heart's content.

Qwilleran opened the wicker hamper in the cats' parlor and invited two reluctant Siamese to jump out. Why, he asked himself, did they never want to get into the hamper? And when they were in it, why did they never want to get out? Koko and Yum Yum finally emerged cautiously, a performance they had repeated every night for the last year, stalking the premises and sniffing the furnishings as if they suspected the room to be bugged or booby-trapped.

"Cats!" Qwilleran said aloud. "Who can understand them?"

He left the Siamese to their own peculiar occupations—licking each other, wrestling, chasing, biting ears, and sniffing indiscreetly—while he tuned in the midnight news in his sitting room.

"The offices and printing plant of the *Pickax Picayune* were destroyed by fire tonight. The building is a total loss, according to fire chief Bruce Scott. Twenty-five fire fighters, three tankers, and two pumpers from Pickax and surrounding communities responded to the alarm and are still on the scene. No injuries have been reported. Elsewhere in the county, the Mooseville Village Council voted to spend five hundred dollars on Christmas decorations—"

He snapped off the radio in exasperation. The

same fifteen-second news item would be repeated hourly without further details. Listeners would not be told how the fire had started, who reported it, what records and equipment had been destroyed, the age of the building, its construction, the problems encountered in fighting the fire, precautions taken, the estimated value of the loss, the insurance coverage.

Without doubt the county needed a newspaper. As for the fate of the *Picayune*, it was regrettable, but one had to be realistic. The *Pic* had been a relic of the horse-and-buggy era. It was Senior's sentimentality and self-indulgence that had bankrupted his newspaper. Typesetting was his obsession, his reason for living, to quote Junior.

Reason for living? Qwilleran jerked to attention and combed his moustache with his fingertips. If the newspaper had truly been on the brink of failure, could Senior's accident have been a suicide? The old plank bridge would be a logical place for a fatal "accident." It was well known to be hazardous. Senior was a cautious, sober man—not one of the Friday-night drunks or speeding youths who usually came to grief at the bridge.

Qwilleran felt a tingling sensation on his upper lip, and he knew his suspicion was valid. There was something uncanny about his upper lip. A tingling, a tremor, or simply a vague uneasiness in the roots of his moustache told him when he was on the right scent. And now he was getting the signal.

If Senior had intended to take his own life, a

staged "accident" would avoid the suicide clause, provided the insurance policy had been in effect long enough. Didn't Junior mention that Grandma Gage had been paying the premiums for years?

An "accident" might pay double indemnity to the widow, or even triple indemnity, although that would be a gamble: There would be a thorough investigation. Insurance companies objected to being fooled.

Perhaps Senior feared something worse than losing the newspaper. He had taken desperate measures to keep the *Picayune* afloat—selling the farmland, mortgaging the farmhouse, begging from his mother-in-law. Did his desperation lead him into something illegal? Did he fear exposure? How about the man in the black raincoat? What was he doing in Pickax? Senior's death had occurred only a few hours before the stranger arrived on the plane. Did Senior know he was coming? And why was the visitor hanging around? Were others implicated?

And now the *Picayune* offices had been destroyed. It was curious timing for such a disaster. Was there something in the basement of the building besides presses and back-copy files? Was it incriminating evidence that had to be eliminated? Who knew what was there? And who threw the match?

Qwilleran roused himself from his reverie and flexed the leg that was going to sleep. He was getting some weird notions. What had Mrs. Cobb put in that cocoa?

From the cats' parlor down the hall came a muf-

fled but recognizable sound: *thlunk!* It was followed
by another *thlunk*—then again *thlunk thlunk thlunk*
in rapid succession. It was the sound of books falling on a carpeted floor. Koko was bumping his private collection.

FOUR

Wednesday, November thirteenth. "Continued cold, with overcast skies and snow showers accumulating to three to four inches."

"Overcast!" Qwilleran bellowed at the radio on his desk. "Why don't you look out the window? The sun's shining like the Fourth of July!"

He turned his attention back to Tuesday's *Daily Fluxion*, which had given good space to the story about the *Pickax Picayune*. It was not entirely accurate, but small towns were glad of any attention at all in the metropolitan press. Then he tried to read about the disasters, terrorism, crime, and graft

Down Below, but his mind kept drifting back to Moose County.

Snow or no snow, he wanted to drive out in the country, look at the old plank bridge, visit the Goodwinter farmhouse, meet the widow. He would take flowers, offer condolences, and ask a few polite questions. It was an approach he had always handled well on the newsbeat. Sad eyes and drooping moustache gave him a mournful demeanor that passed for deep sympathy.

In the county telephone book he found Senior Goodwinter listed on Black Creek Lane in North Middle Hummock. On the county map he could find neither. He found Middle Hummock and West Middle Hummock. He found Mooseville, Smith's Folly, Squunk Corners, Chipmunk, and Brrr, which was not a misprint; the town was the coldest spot in the county. But North Middle Hummock was not to be found. He took his problem to Mr. O'Dell, who knew all the answers.

Mrs. Fulgrove and Mr. O'Dell were the day help at the K mansion. The woman scrubbed and polished six days a week with almost religious fervor; the houseman handled the heavy jobs. Mr. O'Dell had been a school janitor for forty years and had shepherded thousands of students through adolescence—answering their questions, solving their problems, and lending them lunch money. "Janitor" was a revered title in Pickax, and if Mr. O'Dell ever decided to run for the office of mayor, he would be elected unanimously. Now, with his silver hair and ruddy complexion and benign expression, he super-intended the Klingenschoen estate as naturally as he had supervised the education of Pickax youth.

Qwilleran found the houseman lubricating the hinges on the broom closet door. "Do you know the location of Senior Goodwinter's farmhouse, Mr. O'Dell? I don't find North Middle Hummock on the map."

In a lilting voice the houseman said, "The divil himself couldn't find the likes o' that on the map, I'm thinkin', for it's a ghost town fifty year since, but yourself can find it, for I'm after tellin' you how to get there. Go east, now, past the Buckshot Mine, where the wind will be whistlin' in the mine shaft on a day without wind, and there'll be moanin' from the lower depths. When you come to the old plank bridge, let you be wary, for the boards rattle like the divil's own teeth. Keep watch for a lonely tree on a high hill—the hangin' tree, they're callin' it—for then you're comin' to the church where me and my colleen got ourselves married by the good Father Ryan forty-five year since, God rest her soul. And when you come to a deal o' rubble, that's all that's left o' North Middle Hummock."

"I feel we're getting warm," Qwilleran said.

"Warm, is it? There's a ways to go yet—two miles till you set eyes on Captain Fugtree's farm with the white fence. Beyond the sheep meadow pay no mind to the sign sayin' Fugtree Sideroad, for it's Black Creek Lane, and the Goodwinter house you'll be seein' at the end of it. Gray, it is, with a yellow door."

As Qwilleran set out for a North Middle Hummock that didn't exist and a Black Creek Lane that was called something else, he marveled at the information programmed in the heads of Moose County natives for instant retrieval. If Mr. O'Dell could recite the directions in such detail, Senior Goodwinter, who had driven the tortuous route every day, would know every jog in the road, every pothole, every patch of loose gravel. It was not likely that Senior had wrecked his car accidentally.

Qwilleran heard no whistling or moaning at the Buckshot Mine, but the old plank bridge did indeed rattle ominously. Although the parapets were built of stone, the roadbed was a loose strip of lateral planks. The "hanging tree" was well named—an ancient gnarled oak making a grotesque silhouette against the sky. Everything else checked out: the church, the rubble, the white fence, the sheep meadow.

The farmhouse at the end of Black Creek Lane was a rambling structure of weathered gray shingles, set in a yard covered with the gold and red leaves of maples. Clumps of chrysanthemums were still blooming stubbornly around the doorstep.

Qwilleran lifted a brass door knocker shaped like the Greek letter *pi* and let it drop on the yellow door. He had taken the risk of dropping in without an appointment, country style, and when the door opened he was greeted without surprise by a pleasant young woman in a western shirt.

"I'm Jim Qwilleran," he said. "I couldn't attend the funeral, but I've brought some flowers for Mrs. Goodwinter."

"I know you!" she exclaimed. "I used to see your picture in the *Daily Fluxion* before I moved to Montana. Come right in!" She turned and shouted up the staircase. "Mother! You've got company!"

The woman who came down the stairs was no distraught widow with eyes red from weeping and sleeplessness; she was a hearty type in a red warm-up suit, with eyes sparkling and cheeks pink as if she had just come in from jogging.

"Mr. Qwilleran!" she cried with outstretched hand. "How good of you to drop in! We've all read your column in the *Fluxion*, and we're so glad you're living up here."

He presented the flowers. "With my compliments and sympathy, Mrs. Goodwinter."

"Please call me Gritty. Everyone does," she said. "And thank you for your kindness. Roses! I love roses! Let's go into the keeping room. Every other place is torn up for inventory. . . . Pug, honey, put these lovely flowers in a vase, will you? That's a dear."

The hundred-year-old farmhouse had many small rooms with wide floorboards and six-over-six windows with some of the original wavy glass. The mismatched furnishings were obviously family heirlooms, but the interior was self-consciously coordinated: blue-and-white tiles, blue-and-white calico curtains, and blue-and-white china on the plate rail. Antique cooking utensils hung in and around the large fireplace.

Gritty said, "We've been hoping you would join the country club, Mr. Qwilleran."

"I haven't done any joining," he said, "because I'm concentrating on writing a book."

"Not about Pickax, I hope," the widow said with a laugh. "It would be banned in Boston.... Pug, honey, bring us a drink, will you? ... What will you have, Mr. Qwilleran?"

"Ginger ale, club soda, anything like that. And everyone calls me Qwill."

"How about a Coke with a little rum?" She was tempting him with a sidelong glance. "Live it up, Qwill!"

"Thanks, but I've been on the wagon for several years."

"Well, you're doing *something* right! You look wonderfully healthy." She appraised him from head to foot. "Are you happy in Moose County?"

"I'm getting used to it—the fresh air, the relaxed lifestyle, the friendly people," he said. "It must be a comfort to you, during this sad time, to have so many friends and relatives."

"The relatives you can have!" she said airily. "But, yes—I am fortunate to have good friends."

Her daughter brought a tray of beverages, and Qwilleran raised his glass. "With hope for the future!"

"You're so right!" said his hostess, flourishing a double old-fashioned. "Would you stay for lunch, Qwill? I've made a ham-and-spinach quiche with funeral leftovers. Pug, honey, see if it's ready to come out of the oven. Stick a knife in it."

The visit was not what Qwilleran had anticipated. He was required to shift abruptly from condolence to social chitchat. "You have a beautiful house," he remarked.

"It may look good," Gritty said, "but it's a pain in the you-know-what. I'm tired of floors that slope and doors that creak and septic tanks that back up and stairs with narrow treads. God! They must have had small feet in the old days. And small bottoms! Look at those Windsor chairs! I'm selling the house and moving to an apartment in Indian Village—near the golf course, you know."

Pug said, "Mother is a champion golfer. She wins all the tournaments."

"What will you do with your antiques when you move?" Qwilleran asked innocently.

"Sell them at auction. Do you like auctions? They're the major pastime in Moose County—next to potluck suppers and messing around."

"Oh, *Mother*!" Pug remonstrated. She turned to Qwilleran. "That big rolltop desk belonged to my great-grandfather. He founded the *Picayune*."

"It looks like a rolltop coffin," her mother said. "I've been doomed to live with antiques all my life. Never liked them. Crazy, isn't it?"

Lunch was served at a pine table in the kitchen, and the quiche arrived on blue-and-white plates.

Gritty said, "I hope this is the last meal I ever eat on blue china. It makes food look yukky, but the whole set was handed down in my husband's family—hundreds of pieces that refuse to break."

"I was appalled," Qwilleran said, "when the *Picayune* offices burned down. I was hoping the paper would continue to publish under Junior's direction."

"Pooh on the *Picayune*," said Gritty. "They should have pulled the plug thirty years ago."

"But it's unique in the annals of journalism. Junior could have carried on the tradition, even if they printed the paper by modern methods."

"No," she said. "That boy will marry his midget, and they'll both leave Pickax and go Down Below to get jobs. Probably in a sideshow," she added with a laugh. "Junior is the runt of the litter."

"Oh, *Mother*, don't say such things," Pug protested. To Qwilleran she said, "Mother is the humorist in the family."

"It hides my broken heart," the widow said with a debonair shrug.

"What will happen to the *Picayune* building now? Were they able to salvage anything?"

"It's all gone," she said without apparent regret. "The building is gutted, but the stone walls are okay. They're two feet thick. It would make a good minimall with six or eight shops, but we'll have to wait and see what we collect on insurance."

Throughout the visit thoughts were racing

through Qwilleran's mind: Everything was being done too fast; it all seemed beautifully planned. As for the widow, either she was braving it out or she was utterly heartless. "Gritty" affected him less like a courageous woman and more like the sand in the spinach quiche.

Returning home, he telephoned Dr. Zoller's dental clinic and spoke with the young receptionist who had such dazzlingly capped teeth.

"This is Jim Qwilleran, Pam. Could I get an appointment this afternoon to have my teeth cleaned?"

"One moment. Let me find your card.... You were here in July, Mr. Q. You're not due until January."

"This is an emergency. I've been drinking a lot of tea."

"Oh.... Well, in that case you're in luck. Jody just had a cancellation. Can you come right over?"

"In three minutes and twenty seconds." In Pickax one was never more than five minutes away from anywhere.

The clinic occupied a lavishly renovated stone stable that had once been a ten-cent barn behind the old Pickax Hotel in horse-and-buggy days. Jody greeted Qwilleran eagerly. In her long white coat she looked even more diminutive.

"I've been trying to reach you!" she said. "Juney wants you to know that he's flying Down Below to see the editor who promised him a job. He left at noon."

"Well, that's the end of the old *Picayune*," Qwilleran said.

"Fasten your seat belt. You're going for a ride." She adjusted the dental chair to its lowest level. "Is your head comfy?"

"How late did Junior stay at the fire scene?"

"He got in at five-thirty this morning, and he was beat! They had to stay and watch for hot spots, you know. . . . Now open wide."

"Salvage anything?" he asked quickly before complying.

"I don't think so. The papers that weren't burned were soaked. As soon as they knocked the fire down they let Juney go in with an air pack to see if he could find a fireproof box that belonged to his dad. But the smoke was too thick. He couldn't even *see*—Oops! Did I puncture you?"

"Arrh," Qwilleran replied with his mouth full of instruments.

Jody's tiny fingers had a delicate touch, but her hands were shaking after a sleepless night.

"Juney says they don't know what caused the fire. He didn't let anyone smoke when they were taking pictures. . . . Is that a sensitive spot?"

"Arrh arrh."

"Poor Juney! He was crushed—absolutely crushed! He's really not strong enough to be a nozzleman, you know, but the chief let him take the hose—with three backup men instead of two. It made Juney feel—not so helpless, you know. . . . Now you can rinse out."

"Building well insured?"

"Just a tad wider, please. That's it! . . . There's some insurance, but most of the stuff is priceless, because it's old and irreplaceable. . . . Now rinse."

"Too bad the old issues weren't on microfilm and stored somewhere for safety."

"Juney said it would cost too much money."

"Who reported the fire?" Another quick question between rinses.

"Some kids cruising on Main Street. They saw smoke, and when the trucks got there, the whole building was in flames. . . . Is this hurting you?"

"Arrh arrh."

She sighed. "So I guess Juney will take a job at the *Fluxion*, and his mother will sell everything." She whipped off the bib. "There you go! Have you been flossing after every meal like Dr. Zoller told you?"

"Inform Dr. Zoller," Qwilleran said, "that not only do I floss after meals but I floss between the courses. In restaurants I'm known as the Mad Flosser."

From the dental clinic he went to Scottie's Men's Shop. Qwilleran, whose mother had been a Mackintosh, was partial to Scots, and the storekeeper had a brogue that he turned on for good customers.

Throughout his career Qwilleran had never cared much about clothes, being satisfied with a drab uniform of coat, pants, shirt, and tie. There was something about the north-country lifestyle, however, that sparked his interest in tartan shirts, Icelandic sweaters, shearling parkas, trooper hats, bulky boots, and buckskin choppers. And the more Scottie burred his *r*'s, the more Qwilleran bought.

Entering the store, Qwilleran said, "What happened to the four inches of snow we were supposed to get today?"

"All bosh," said Scottie, shaking his shaggy head of gray hair. "Canna believe a worrrd of what they say on radio. A body can get better information from the woolly caterpillars."

"You look as if you lost some sleep last night."

"Aye, it were a bad one, verra bad," said the volunteer fire chief. "Didna get home till six this mornin'. Chipmunk and Kennebeck sent crews to help. Couldna do it without 'em—or without our women, God bless 'em. Kept the coffee and sandwiches comin' all night."

"How did Junior take it?"

"It were hard on the lad. Many a time I been in the newspaper office to pass the time o' day with his old man. A fire trap, it was! Tons of paper! And them old wood partitions—dry as tinder—and the old wood floor!" Scottie shook his head again.

"Any idea how it started?"

"Couldna say. They'd been takin' pictures, and it could be a careless cigarette smolderin'. There's a flammable solvent they always used for cleanin' the old presses, and when it hit, it raced like wildfire."

"Any suspicion of arson?"

"No evidence of monkey business. No reason to bring the marshal up here to my way o' thinkin'."

"But you saved the lodge hall and post office, Scottie."

"Aye, we did indeed, but it were touch an' go."

On the way home Qwilleran stopped at the public library to check the reading room. The man who claimed to be a historian was not there, and the clerks had not seen him since Tuesday morning. Polly Duncan was not there either, and the clerks said she had left for the day.

For dinner that night Mrs. Cobb served beef Stroganoff and poppy-seed noodles, and after second helpings and a wedge of pumpkin pie, Qwilleran took some out-of-town newspapers and two new magazines into the library. He drew the draperies and touched a match to Mr. O'Dell's expert arrangement of split logs, kindling, and paper twists. Then he sprawled in his favorite lounge chair and propped his feet on the ottoman.

The Siamese immediately presented themselves. They knew a fire was being lighted before the woodsy aroma circulated, before the crackle of the kindling, even before the match was struck. After washing up in the warmth of the blaze, Koko started nosing books and Yum Yum jumped on Qwilleran's lap, turning around three times before settling down.

The female was developing an inordinate affection for the man. She was brazenly possessive of his lap. She gazed at him with adoring eyes, purred when he looked her way, and liked nothing better than to reach up and touch his moustache with a velvet paw. True, he called her his little sweetheart, but her obsessive desire for propinquity was disturbing. He had mentioned it to Lori Bamba, the young woman who knew all about cats.

"They go for the opposite sex," Lori explained, "and they know which is which. It's hard to explain."

Yum Yum was dozing on his lap, a picture of catly contentment, when Qwilleran heard the first *thlunk*. There was no sense in scolding Koko. It went in one pointed ear and out the other. When reprimanded in the past, he had not only resented it; he had found his own ingenious way of retaliation. In any argument, Qwilleran had learned, a Siamese always has the last word.

So he merely sighed, transferred his lapful of sleeping fur to the ottoman, and went to see what damage had been done. As he expected, it was Shakespeare again. Mrs. Fulgrove had been rubbing the pigskin bindings with a mixture of lanolin and neat's-foot oil, to preserve the leather, and both ingredients were animal products. But whatever the explanation for Koko's special interest in these books, two of them were now on the floor, and they happened to be Qwilleran's favorite plays: *Macbeth* and *Julius Caesar*.

He leafed through the latter until he found a passage he liked: the conspiracy scene, in which men plotting to assassinate Caesar meet under cover of darkness, shadowing their faces with their cloaks.

"And let us bathe our hands in Caesar's blood up to the elbows, and besmear our swords."

Conspiracy, Qwilleran reflected, was Shakespeare's favorite device for establishing conflict, creating suspense, and grabbing the emotions of the audience. In *Macbeth* there was the conspiracy to murder the old king. *"Who would have thought the old man to have had so much blood in him?"*

A tremor on Qwilleran's upper lip alerted him. Was the *Picayune*'s double tragedy the result of a conspiracy? He had no clues—only the sensation in the roots of his moustache. He had no clues and no logical way to investigate.

Years before, as a prize-winning crime reporter, he had developed a network of anonymous sources. In Moose County he had no sources. Although the natives were notorious gossips, they avoided gossiping with outsiders, and Qwilleran was an outsider even after eighteen months in their midst.

He glanced at the calendar. It was Wednesday, November thirteenth. On the evening of November fourteenth he would have seventy-five certified gossips under his roof—all the best people, drinking tea and socializing.

"Okay, old sleuth," he said to Koko. "Tomorrow night we cultivate some sources."

FIVE

Thursday, November fourteenth. The weather was cooperating with the major social event of the season—not too cold, not too windy, not too damp. On Thursday evening seventy-five members of the Historical Society and Old Timers Club would view the Klingenschoen mansion for the first time, and the residence would become officially the Klingenschoen Museum.

Ever since inheriting the pretentious edifice Qwilleran had considered it an absurd residence for a bachelor and two cats. He proposed, therefore—with the cooperation of the Historical Society—to open the mansion to the public as a museum two or three afternoons a week. When the mayor announced the news at a council meeting, the citizens of Pickax were jubilant, and the guests invited to the preview felt singularly honored.

Qwilleran's day began as usual in his garage apartment. He tuned in the weather report, drank a cup of instant coffee, dressed, and walked down the corridor to the cats' parlor.

"Commuter Special now leaving on track four," he announced, opening the wicker hamper.

The Siamese sat nose-to-nose on the windowsill, enjoying the thin glimmer of November sunshine and ignoring the invitation.

"Breakfast now being served in the dining car."

There was no response, not even the flicker of a whisker. Impatiently Qwilleran picked up one animal in each hand and deposited them unceremoniously in the hamper.

"If you act like cats, you get treated like cats," he explained in a reasonable voice. "Act like courteous, cooperative, intelligent beings, and you get treated accordingly."

There were sounds of scuffling and snarling inside the hamper as he carried it across the yard to the main house.

It was Mrs. Cobb's idea that the Siamese should spend their days among the Oriental rugs, French tapestries, and rare old books of the mansion. "When you have valuable antiques," she explained, "you have four things to fear: theft, fire, dry heat, and mice."

At her urging Qwilleran had installed humidity controls, a burglar alarm, smoke detectors, and a direct line to the police station and fire hall. Koko and Yum Yum were expected to handle the other hazards.

When Qwilleran arrived at the back door with the wicker hamper, the housekeeper called out from the kitchen, "Would you like a mushroom omelette, Mr. Q?"

"Sounds fine. I'll feed the cats. What's in the refrigerator?"

"Sautéed chicken livers. Koko would probably prefer them warmed with some of last night's beef Stroganoff. Yum Yum isn't fussy."

After he had finished his own breakfast—a three-egg omelette with two toasted English muffins and some of Mrs. Cobb's wild haw jelly—he said, "Delicious! Best mushroomless mushroom omelette I've ever eaten."

"Oh dear!" The housekeeper covered her face with her hands in embarrassment. "Did I forget the filling? I'm so excited about tonight, I don't know whether I'm coming or going. Aren't you excited, Mr. Q?"

"I feel a faint ripple of anticipation," he said.

"Oh, Mr. Q, you must be kidding! You've worked on this for a year!"

It was true. To prepare the mansion for public use, the attic had been paneled and equipped as a meeting room. A paved parking lot was added behind the carriage house. Engineers from Down Below had installed an elevator. A fire escape was required in the rear. For barrier-free access there were such accommodations as a ramp at the rear entrance, a new bathroom on the main floor, and elevator controls at wheelchair height.

"What's the order of events tonight?" Qwilleran asked Mrs. Cobb. She had chaired the Historical Society committee on arrangements.

"The members will start arriving at seven o'clock for a conducted tour of the museum. Mrs. Exbridge has trained eighteen guides."

"And who trained Mrs. Exbridge? Don't be so modest, Mrs. Cobb. I know and you know that this entire venture would have been impossible without your expertise."

"Oh, thank you, Mr. Q," she said, flushing self-consciously, "but I can't take too much credit. Mrs. Exbridge knows a lot about antiques. She wants to open an antique shop now that her divorce is final."

"Don Exbridge's wife? I didn't know they were having trouble. Sorry to hear it." Qwilleran always empathized with the principals in a divorce case, having survived a painful experience himself.

"Yes, it's too bad," Mrs. Cobb said. "I don't know what went wrong. Susan Exbridge doesn't talk about it. She's a very nice woman. I've never met *him*."

"I've run into him a couple of times. He's an agreeable guy with a smile and a handshake for everyone."

"Well, he's a developer, you know, and I take a

dim view of *them*. We were always fighting developers and bureaucrats Down Below. They wanted to tear down twenty antique shops and some historic houses."

"So what happens after the tour of the museum?"

"We go up to the meeting hall, and that's when you make your speech."

"Not a speech. Just a few words. Please!"

"Then there'll be a brief business meeting and refreshments."

"I hope you didn't bake seventy-five dozen cookies for those shameless cookie hounds," Qwilleran said. "I suspect most of them attend meetings because of your lemon-coconut bars. Will your friend be there?"

"Herb? No, he has to get up early tomorrow morning. It's the start of gun season for deer, you know. How about the cats? Will they attend the preview?"

"Why not? Yum Yum will spend the evening on top of the refrigerator, but Koko likes to parade around and show off."

The telephone rang, and Koko sprang to the desk in the kitchen, as if he knew it was a call from Lori Bamba in Mooseville.

Lori was Qwilleran's part-time secretary, a young woman with long golden braids tied with blue ribbons that tantalized the Siamese.

"Hi, Qwill," she said. "Hope I'm not interrupting something crucial. Isn't this the big day?"

"You're right. Tonight we go public. What's the news from Mooseville?"

"Nick just phoned me from work and said I should call you. Someone's camping on your property at the lake. On his way to work he saw an RV parked in the woods there. He wondered if you had authorized it."

"Don't know a thing about it. But is it all that bad? There's a lot of land there that isn't being used." Qwilleran had inherited the lake property along with the mansion in Pickax: eighty acres of woodland with beach frontage and a log cabin.

"It isn't a good idea to encourage trespassers," Lori said. "They could leave a lot of litter, cut down your trees, set the woods on fire . . ."

"Okay, okay, I'm convinced."

"Nick said you should call the sheriff."

"I'll do that. Appreciate your interest. How's everything in Mooseville? How's the baby?"

"He finally said his first word. He said 'moose' very distinctly, so we think he'll grow up to be president of the Chamber of Commerce. . . . Do I hear Koko talking in the background?"

"He wants to have a few words with you."

Qwilleran held the receiver to Koko's ear, which flicked and swiveled in excitement. There followed a series of "yows" and "iks" and purrs of varying intensity and inflection.

When the conversation ended, Qwilleran said to the housekeeper, "The English language has six hundred thousand words. Koko has only two, but he gets more music and meaning out of 'yow' and 'ik' than some of our learned friends get out of the whole dictionary."

"That Lori certainly has a way with cats," Mrs. Cobb said with a trace of envy.

"If Lori had lived in Salem three hundred years ago, she would have been burned at the stake."

The housekeeper looked saddened. "I don't think Koko likes me."

"Why do you say that, Mrs. Cobb?"

"He never talks to me or purrs or comes to be petted."

"Siamese," Qwilleran began, clearing his throat and selecting his words carefully, "are less demonstrative than other breeds, and Koko in particular is not a lap cat, although I'm sure he likes you."

"Yum Yum rubs against my ankles when I'm cooking and jumps on my lap sometimes. She's a very sweet kitty."

"Koko is less emotional and more cerebral," Qwilleran explained. "He has his own attributes and personality, and we have to understand him and accept him for what he is. He may not make a fuss over you, but he respects you and appreciates the wonderful food you prepare."

He extricated himself from this ticklish dialogue with a sense of relief. Koko had alienated more than one woman of his acquaintance, and a standoff between a temperamental cat and a superlative housekeeper was much to be avoided.

From the library he telephoned the sheriff's office,

and within a half hour there was a brown uniform at the back door.

"Sheriff's department, sir," said the deputy. "Got a report on the radio about your property east of Mooseville. No RV in your woods, sir, although there were recent tire tracks and a couple of empty cigarette packs. He buried the butts, so he knows something about camping. They were Canadian cigarettes. We get a lot of Canadian tourists here. No sign of poaching. No break-in or vandalism at your cabin. Gun season starts tomorrow, sir. If you don't want trespassers with rifles, you ought to have your property posted."

The day wore on. The weather held. Excitement mounted. Mrs. Cobb put sugar in the soup and salt in the applesauce. Koko's tail was stepped on twice.

At seven o'clock every light in the mansion was turned on. Eighty tall narrow windows glowing with light on a wintry night created a spectacle that Pickax had never before seen, and traffic cruised around the Park Circle to gawk.

When the guests arrived they were greeted by Qwilleran and the officers of the Historical Society. Then they moved from room to room, marveling at the richness and palatial dimensions of the interior. The drawing room, with its twin fireplaces and twin chandeliers, had a fortune in oil paintings on the crimson damask walls. The dining room, designed to seat sixteen, was paneled in carved walnut imported from England in the nineteenth century. The visitors were so entranced by the museum that

Koko went unnoticed, although he strutted in their midst and struck statuesque poses on the carved newel post and the antique rosewood piano.

At eight o'clock the meeting was called to order in the third-floor assembly room. Nigel Fitch, a trust officer at the bank, rapped the gavel and asked everyone to rise for a moment of silent tribute to Senior Goodwinter. Then the thanking began. First the president thanked the weatherman for postponing the snow. He thanked Qwilleran for making the mansion available as a museum.

Qwilleran rose and thanked the society members for their encouragement and support. He thanked XYZ Enterprises for donating labor for the construction projects. He thanked the CPA firm for computerizing the museum catalogue. Particularly he thanked Mrs. Cobb for establishing the museum on a professional level. Then she thanked the four committees that had worked on the preview. The president kept glancing toward the elevator expectantly.

During the transaction of old and new business Polly Duncan, representing the public library, proposed an oral history project to preserve the recollections of Old Timers on tape. "It should be handled by someone with interviewing skills," she specified, glancing at Qwilleran. He said he might give it a try.

Nigel Fitch, who usually chaired a brisk meeting, was proceeding at a leisurely pace. "We're expecting the mayor," he explained, "but he's been delayed at the city hall."

Whenever Fitch glanced toward the elevator, all heads in the audience turned hopefully in the same direction. At one point there were mechanical sounds in the elevator shaft, and a hush fell in the meeting hall. The doors opened, and out stepped an Old Timer, tall and thin and nattily dressed. He gave the president a cheerful salute and walked to an empty seat with a disjointed gait, like a robot.

"That's Mr. Tibbitt," whispered a woman next to Qwilleran. "A retired school principal. He's ninety-three. A dear old man."

"Mr. President," said Susan Exbridge, "I would like to make a proposal. The Singing Society will present Handel's *Messiah* at the Old Stone Church on November twenty-fourth, exactly as it was performed in the eighteenth century, with singers in period costume. We had planned a reception for the performers afterward, and this museum would be a marvelous place to have it, if Mr. Qwilleran would consent."

"Okay with me," said Qwilleran, "provided I don't have to wear satin knee breeches."

And still the mayor did not arrive. Looking frequently at his watch, Fitch invited discussions on raising the dues, recruiting new members, and starting a newsletter.

Finally the telltale hum in the elevator shaft was heard, followed by a click as the car reached the third floor. All heads turned in anticipation. The elevator door opened, and out walked Koko—his tail perpendicular, his ears proudly erect, and a dead mouse gripped in his jaws.

Qwilleran jumped to his feet. "And I want to thank the vice president in charge of extermination for his diligence in eliminating certain museum hazards."

"Meeting adjourned," shouted Fitch.

During the social hour the banker said to Qwilleran, "That's a remarkable cat you have. How did he do it?"

Qwilleran explained that Mr. O'Dell was downstairs, and he had probably put Koko in the car, pressed the button, and sent him up—for laughs.

Actually Qwilleran thought nothing of the kind. Koko was capable of boarding the car, stretching to his full length, and reaching the controls with a paw. He had done it before. The cat was fascinated by push buttons, keys, levers, and knobs. But how could one explain that to a banker?

When the mayor finally arrived, he cornered Qwilleran. "Say, Qwill, when is this town going to emerge from the Dark Ages?"

"What do you mean?"

"Did you ever hear of a whole county trying to function without a newspaper? We all knew Senior was a nut, but we thought Junior would take over and make it go. He's a bright kid; I had him in poli sci when I was teaching. But I suppose you've heard Gritty's selling the *Picayune* to you-know-who. They'll make a mint of money on it—as an ad sheet, that's all—and we still won't have any news coverage. Why don't you start a paper, Qwill?"

"Well, it's like this. I used to think I'd like to own my own newspaper and my own four-star restaurant and my own big-league ball club, but I've had to face the fact that I'm not a financier or an administrator."

"Okay. How about your connections Down Below? I know you lured that young couple up here to turn the Old Stone Mill around."

"I'll think about it," Qwilleran promised.

"Think fast."

Over the cups of weak tea and mildly alcoholic punch there was no lack of chatter:

"Incredible collection of antiques!"

"How do you like this weather?"

"A memorable evening! We are indebted to you, Mr. Qwilleran."

"Snow's never been so late."

"What are you doing for Thanksgiving?"

"Would you like a twelve-foot Christmas tree for the museum, Qwill? I have a beauty on my farm."

"Charming place for a wedding. My son is being married soon."

There were no theories about Senior's accident or the *Picayune* fire, however, despite Qwilleran's leading questions. He was still an outsider. Although an eavesdropper by profession, he heard nothing that suggested illegal activity or conspiracy.

While he felt an underlying disappointment, he noticed that Mrs. Cobb was unusually elated. She talked vivaciously, laughed much, and accepted compliments without blushing. Something wonderful had happened to her, he guessed. She had won the state lottery, or she was a grandmother for the first time, or the mayor had appointed her to the Commission on Preservation. Whatever the reason, Mrs. Cobb was inordinately happy.

Then Qwilleran observed a pair of Old Timers sitting in a corner with their heads together. A frail woman dependent upon a walker was listening to an old man with a cane as he talked about the *Picayune* fire. Qwilleran inquired if they were enjoying the party.

"Good cookies," said the man, "but they shoulda put somethin' in the punch. Glad it didn't snow."

"We don't get out much after snow flies," said his companion. "I never saw such a grand house!"

"Couldn't hear a word at the meeting, though."

The woman sniffed. "Amos, you always sit in the back row, and you always complain you can't hear."

Qwilleran asked their names.

"I'm Amos Cook, eighty-eight," the man said. "Eighty-eight and still cookin'. Heh heh heh." He jerked his thumb. "She's a young chick, eighty-five. Heh heh heh."

"I'm Hettie Spence, and I'll be eighty-six next month," she said. The Old Timers flaunted their ages like medals. "I was a Fugtree before I married Mr. Spence. He had the hardware store. We raised five children of our own—four of them boys—and three foster children. They all went to college. My eldest son is an ophthalmologist Down Below." She spoke with a fluttering of eyelids, hands, and shoulders.

"My grand-niece married one o' them," Amos put in.

"I wrote the obituaries for the *Picayune* before my arthritis got too bad," Hettie said. "I wrote the obituary for the last of the Klingenschoens."

"I read it," said Qwilleran. "It was unforgettable."

"My father wouldn't let me go away to college, but I took correspondence courses, and—"

Amos interrupted. "Her and me was in the pictures they took before the fire."

"How did you enjoy it?" Qwilleran asked. "Was the photographer good? How many pictures did she take?"

"Too many," he complained. "I got awful tired. I just had a gall bladder operation. She went click-click-click. Not like the old days. In them days you had to watch the birdie till your face froze, and the man had his head under a black cloth."

"In those days we had to say 'plum' before he snapped the picture," Hettie said. "We never had girl photographers then."

"Wouldn't let me smoke my corncob. Said it would fog up the pictures. Never heard anythin' so silly."

Qwilleran asked what time they left the newspaper office.

"My grandson picked us up at six," Amos said.

"Five," Hettie corrected him.

"Six, Hettie. Junior took the girl to the airport at half past five."

"Well, my watch said five, and I took my medication."

"You forgot to wind it, and you took your pill too late. That's why you got a dizzy spell."

Qwilleran interrupted. "And the fire broke out about four hours later. Do you have any idea what caused it?"

The old couple looked at each other and shook their heads.

"How long had you worked at the *Picayune*, Mr. Cook?"

"I was a printer's devil when I was ten, and I stayed till I couldn't work no more." He patted his chest. "Weak ticker. But I got to be head pressman when Titus was alive. We had two men and a boy on them handpresses, and it took all day to print a couple of thousand. The paper sold for a penny then. You could get a whole year for a dollar."

Qwilleran remembered the book Polly had given him. "Would you good people come downstairs and look at an old picture of *Picayune* employees? You might be able to identify them."

"My eyes aren't very good," Hettie said. "Cataracts. And I don't move so fast since I broke my hip."

Nevertheless, Qwilleran conducted them to the library and produced his copy of *Picturesque Pickax*. He flicked on the tape recorder, and the interview was later transcribed by Lori Bamba.

Question: This is a picture of Picayune *employees, taken sometime before 1921. Do you recognize any of the faces?*

Amos: I'm not in the picture. Don't even know when it was took. But that's Titus Goodwinter in the middle—the one with the derby hat and handlebar moustache.

Hettie: He always wore a derby hat. Who's that next to Titus?

Amos: The one with arm garters? Don't know him.

Hettie: Was he the bookkeeper?

Amos: No, the bookkeeper has those black things on his sleeves. Bill Watkins, his name was.

Hettie: Bill was the sheriff. His cousin Barnaby kept books. I went to school with him. He was killed by a runaway horse and wagon.

Amos: It was the sheriff that tried to stop a runaway, Hettie. Barnaby was shot in the head with a rifle.

Hettie: I beg to differ. Barnaby didn't believe in firearms. I knew his whole family.

Amos: (loudly) I didn't say he had a gun! Some hunter shot him!

Hettie: I thought the sheriff always carried a gun.

Amos: (louder) We're talking about the bookkeeper! Barnaby! The one with black sleeve things!

Hettie: Don't shout!

Amos: Well, anyway, the one with the derby hat is Titus Goodwinter.

Was Titus the founder of the newspaper?

Amos: Nope. Ephraim started the paper way back. Don't know when. Had a big funeral when he died. Hung himself.

Hettie: Ephraim *hanged* himself, or so they said.

Amos: On a big oak tree near the old plank bridge.

Is that when Titus started to manage the newspaper?

Amos: No, the oldest boy took over, but he got throwed by a horse.

Hettie: Millions of blackbirds rose out of a cornfield, and his horse bolted.

Amos: The blackbirds in them days was like the mosquitoes we got now.

Hettie: Titus ran the paper after that. My, he was spoiled! Once when the creek was swollen, his horse wouldn't cross it, and Titus jumped off in a rage and shot him.

Amos: His own horse! Shot him dead! That's Titus in a derby hat. Always wore a derby hat.

Who's the fierce-looking man at the end of the row?

Amos: That's the fellah that drove the wagon, eh, Hettie?

Hettie: That's Zack, all right. I never liked him. He drank.

Amos: Killed Titus in a fight and went to

prison. Good driver, though. Had a pretty daughter. Ellie, her name was. Worked at the paper for a spell.

Hettie: Ellie folded papers and made tea and swept up.

Amos: Threw herself in the river one dark night.

Hettie: Poor girl had no mother, and her father drank, and her brother was a bully.

Amos: Titus took a shine to her.

Hettie: He was always a ladies' man—him and that derby hat and big moustache.

End of interview.

Nigel Fitch interrupted the dialogue, saying he was ready to drive the two Old Timers home. All the guests were drifting out, reluctantly. Plucking Polly from the departing crowd, Qwilleran invited her to stay for an afterglow.

"One little glass of sherry, and then I must leave," she said as they went into the library. "Did you object to my involving you in the oral history project?"

"Not at all. It might prove interesting. Did you know that Senior's father was murdered and his grandfather hanged himself?"

"The family has had a violent history, but you must remember that this was pioneer country like the old Wild West, but at a later date. We're more civilized now."

"Computers and video recorders do not a civilization make."

"That's not Shakespeare, Qwill."

"I visited Mrs. Goodwinter yesterday," he said. "She was hardly one of your traditional widows, ravaged by grief and sedated by the family physician."

"She's a courageous woman. When they named her Gritty, they had reason."

"She's made some rather sudden decisions—to sell the house, auction the furnishings, and let the antique presses go for scrap metal. It's less than a week since Senior died, and the auction posters are all over town. That's too fast."

"People who have never been widowed are always telling widows how to behave," Polly said. "Gritty is a strong woman, like her mother. Euphonia Gage should be on your list for an oral history interview."

"What do you know about XYZ Enterprises?"

"Only that they're successful at everything they undertake."

"Do you know the principals?"

"Slightly. Don Exbridge is a charming man. He's the promoter, the idea person. Caspar Young is the contractor. Dr. Zoller is the financial backer."

"That figures. I suspect he's made a fortune in dental floss," Qwilleran said. "Do X, Y, and Z all belong to the country club?"

He had made a study of the clique system in Pickax. Everything depended on which club one joined, which church one attended, and how long one's family had lived in Moose County. The Goodwinters went back five generations; the Fitches, four.

"I must leave now," said Polly, "before my landlord calls the sheriff and they send out the search posse. Mr. MacGregor is a nice old man, and I don't want to upset him."

After she left, Qwilleran wondered if the fine hand of XYZ Enterprises had guided Mrs. Goodwinter's decisions. They all belonged to the club. They golfed. They played cards. That was the way it worked.

He also wondered if Polly really had an elderly landlord named MacGregor monitoring her activities. Or was it a manufactured excuse for leaving early? And why was she so reluctant to stay late? She was afraid of something. Gossip, perhaps. Pickax imposed a Victorian code of propriety on its professional women, and they took pains to preserve appearances, even though they were privately living in the late twentieth century. Polly's landlord, Qwilleran suspected, might be more than a landlord.

SIX

Friday, November fifteenth. It was the opening day of gun season for deer hunters. At the Klingenschoen Museum it was the morning after the preview, and Mrs. Cobb was still elated and a trifle giddy.

Qwilleran complimented her on the success of the evening. "Everyone praised the museum and the refreshments, not necessarily in that order," he said. "We've been offered a twelve-foot Christmas tree for the foyer, and the Fitches would like to use the museum for their son's wedding."

"It would be a beautiful setting for a wedding,"

she said, adding playfully, "Koko could be ring bearer and carry the ring on his tail."

"You're making jokes this morning," Qwilleran said. "You must be feeling good."

She looked at him coyly. "What would you think about having two weddings here?"

"*You?*"

Her eyes were glowing behind the thick lenses. "Herb is buying a hundred-year-old farmhouse. He called me just before the preview and said he thought we should get married."

"Hmff," Qwilleran said, then searched for something more agreeable to say. "It's the Goodwinter place. I've seen it. It's a gem!"

"He got a good buy because she's in a hurry to sell before snow flies."

"It's overdecorated, but you'd know how to correct that."

"It will be fun to restore it and furnish it with primitives."

"Does Hackpole like antiques?" Qwilleran asked dubiously.

"Not really, but he says I can do anything I want. His chief interest is hunting and fishing. He has cabinets full of guns and hunting knives and fishing rods. He wants to give me a rifle—a .22 rimfire, whatever that is—for squirrels and rabbits." Her pursed lips expressed disapproval.

"It's hard to imagine you tramping around the woods, taking shots at small animals, Mrs. Cobb."

She shuddered. "Herb was telling me how he

field-dresses a deer, and it turned my stomach. By the way, he wants to know if you like venison. He always gets his buck, and he says the meat is delicious if the deer bleeds to death slowly. The heart should keep pumping blood out of the tissues." She quoted without enthusiasm.

"Hmff," Qwilleran said again, his down-turned moustache drooping more than usual. He was not happy with the turn of events. A housekeeper who worked an eight-hour shift and then went home to cook for her husband would be quite different from the live-in housekeeper who had spoiled him and the cats with her cooking during the last eighteen months. Yet he knew that Iris Cobb, twice widowed, yearned for a husband. Too bad she hadn't found one better than Hackpole.

True, he made a good living—in used cars, auto repair, welding, and scrap metal. True, he was a volunteer fire fighter, and that was to his credit. He had fabricated Mrs. Cobb's mobile herb garden in his welding shop; he had picked the berries for her wild haw jelly; he was an expert woodsman. Yet, all around town Hackpole was considered obnoxious. He seemed to have no friends, except Mrs. Cobb, and this inept Romeo now wanted to give her a .22 rifle! Poor woman! She had hoped for a certain expensive silk blouse for her birthday, and Hackpole had given her an expensive Swiss army knife. The man aroused Qwilleran's curiosity.

How had he arranged the purchase of the Good-winter house so fast? He was hardly a member of the country club clique, but he might have connections with XYZ Enterprises. His welding shop probably had the contract for the balcony railings on the Mooseville Motel and the Indian Village units.

Then the telephone rang, and Qwilleran took the call in the library.

A little-girl voice said, "Mr. Qwilleran, this is Jody. Juney came back from Down Below last night. He didn't get hired."

"Did he see the managing editor?"

"Yes, the man who promised him a job. He said they'd just hired three new women reporters and there was no opening at the present time, but they'd keep him in mind."

"Typical!" Qwilleran muttered. "Typical of that guy."

"Juney tried the *Morning Rampage*, too, but they're cutting down their staff. He's terribly depressed. He got in late last night and didn't sleep at all."

"With his academic record he'll have no trouble getting located, Jody. Newspapers send scouts to college campuses every spring to recruit top students. He's tried only one city. He should start cranking out résumés to mail around the country."

"That's what I told him, but he wouldn't listen. He left early this morning and said he was going hunting. He said he'd go to the farmhouse and pick up his brother's rifle—if his mother hasn't sold it already. That's why I'm worried. Juney isn't much of a woodsman, and he isn't crazy about hunting."

"Just getting out in the woods will be good therapy, Jody. It'll sharpen his perspective. And the weather's not bad. Don't worry about him."

"Well, I don't know . . ."

"When Junior gets back, we'll get together and have a talk."

Qwilleran had made an afternoon appointment with Junior's Grandma Gage for an oral history interview, but he had an hour to kill, and he felt restless. Mrs. Cobb's announcement had distressed him, and Junior's disappointment made him vaguely uncomfortable, so he took his own advice: He drove out into the country.

It was a gray day, not likely to cheer one up, and without snow the terrain looked dreary. Traveling north to Mooseville, through good hunting country, he glanced down side roads, looking for Junior's car. Here and there a hunter's car or pickup was parked well off the shoulder in a desolate wooded area, but there was no sign of a red Jaguar. He caught glimpses of a blaze-orange figure crouching in a cornfield or entering the woods, and he heard rifle shots. He was glad he had worn his own blaze-orange cap.

Arriving at his property on the lakeshore, he followed the winding dirt road that led to the cabin. He saw the tire tracks where the camper had parked. Then he went up to the log cabin overlooking the lake. With the windows shuttered, power turned off, and water system drained, it was colder inside than

out. On the beach the snow fences were in position.
The lake looked grim and ready to freeze. Altogether
the scene was bleak and lonely. He heard rifle shots
in the woods and hurried back to his car.

On the way to his appointment with Euphonia
Gage he took a detour down MacGregor Road,
looking for the cottage where Polly claimed to be
living under the watchful eye of her elderly landlord. There were no habitations on this country
road—just open fields interspersed with patches of
woods. There was no traffic except for one car with
a buck tied to the roof. The driver gave Qwilleran a
happy grin and a **V** sign.

Suddenly there was a jog in the road, and the
pavement gave way to gravel. A little farther on,
two mailboxes on cedar posts marked a long driveway bordered with shrubs. It led to a cluster of
buildings: a substantial stone farmhouse, a tiny
frame cottage in the rear, some sheds, and a weathered barn sagging limply to the ground. The names
on the mailboxes were MacGregor and Duncan.

No car was in sight. No farm machinery. No
barking dog. But a goose rounded a corner of the
main house and honked in a menacing manner.
With extreme caution and with one eye on the bird,
Qwilleran stepped out of the car and moved toward
the side door of the farmhouse. There was no need
to knock. He had already been announced.

"What do you want?" screamed a querulous
voice. An old man, frail and stooped, appeared in

the doorway, wearing three sweaters and some knitted leg warmers over his trousers.

"Mr. MacGregor? I'm Jim Qwilleran. Just want to ask you a question, sir."

"What are you selling? I don't want to buy anything."

"I'm not a salesman. I'm looking for a hunter who drives a red Jaguar."

"Red what?"

"A red car. Bright red."

"I don't know," the old man said. "I'm color-blind."

"Thank you anyway, Mr. MacGregor. Good day."

Still watching the goose, Qwilleran backed away. He had determined that Polly really lived in a cottage adjoining a farmhouse belonging to an elderly landlord named MacGregor. Satisfied, he drove back to town. The cottage, he remarked, was incredibly small.

At two-thirty he rang the doorbell of a large stone house on Goodwinter Boulevard, to interview the eighty-two-year-old president of the Old Timers Club. The woman who came to the door was the right age, but he doubted that she could do head-stands and push-ups.

"Mrs. Gage is in her studio," the woman said. "You can go right in—through the front parlor."

A gloomy cave of dark velvet, heavy carved furniture, and black horsehair upholstery led into a light, bright studio, unfurnished except for two large mirrors and an exercise mat. A little woman in leotard, tights, and leg warmers sat in lotus position on the mat. She rose effortlessly and came forward.

"Mr. Qwilleran! I've heard so much about you from Junior! And of course I've read your column in the *Fluxion*." Her voice was calm but vibrant. She threw on a baggy knee-length sweater and led him back into the suffocating front parlor.

She was petite but not frail, white haired but smooth skinned.

"I understand you're president of the Old Timers Club," he said.

"Yes, I'm eighty-two. The youngest member is automatically appointed president."

"I suspect you lied about your age."

Her pleased expression acknowledged the compliment. "I intend to live to be a hundred and three. I think a hundred and four would be excessive, don't you? Exercise is the secret, and *breathing* is the most important factor. Do you know how to *breathe*, Mr. Qwilleran?"

"I've been doing my best for fifty years."

"Stand up and let me place my hands on your rib cage. . . . Now breathe in . . . breathe out . . . inhale . . . exhale. You do very well, Mr. Qwilleran, but you might work on it a little more. Now, what can I do for you?"

"I'd like to turn on this tape recorder and ask you some questions about the early days in Moose County."

"I shall be happy to oblige."

The following interview was later transcribed:

Question: When did your ancestors come to Moose County, Mrs. Gage?

My grandfather came here in the mid-nineteenth century, straight out of medical school. He was the first doctor, and he was treated like a blessing from heaven. There were no hospitals or clinics. Everything was primitive. He made house calls on horseback, sometimes ahead of a pack of howling wolves. And once, after a forest fire, when all the trails were impassable, he chopped his way through fifteen miles of debris with an ax in order to treat the survivors. They were burned and mutilated and blinded, and there were no medicines except what he brought in his knapsack.

What kind of medicines did he have?

Grandfather mixed his own and rolled his own pills, using herbs and botanicals like rhubarb powder and arnica and nux vomica. Some of his patients preferred old-fashioned remedies like catnip tea or a good slug of whiskey. They never paid for his services with money. They'd give him two chickens for setting a broken bone or a bushel of apples for delivering a baby.

What kind of cases did he handle?

Everything. Fever, smallpox, lung disease, surgery, dentistry. He pulled teeth with a pair of "twisters." And there were plenty of emergencies caused by spring floods, poisonous snakes, sawmill accidents, kicking mules, saloon brawls. Amputations were very common. I have his collection of saws, knives, and scalpels.

Why so many amputations?

There were no antibiotics. An infected limb had to be cut off, or the patient would die of blood poisoning. Grandfather talked about performing surgery by candlelight in a log cabin while a member of the family shooed flies away from the open incision. That was over a hundred years ago, you understand. When my father began his practice, conditions had improved. He had an office in our front parlor, and he made house calls in a buggy or sleigh, and he had a full-time driver who lived in the stable and took care of the horses. The driver—Zack was his name—later went to work for the *Picayune* and achieved notoriety by killing Titus Goodwinter.

Do you know the circumstances?

To go back a bit, Zack's father was a miner, blown to bits in an underground explosion. Zack became a bitter and violent man who regularly beat his wife and two children. Father used to patch them up and report it to the constable, but nothing was done about it. Zack's young daughter worked at the *Picayune*, too, and Titus, who was a flagrant roué, seduced the poor girl. She drowned herself, and Zack went after Titus with a hunting knife. Not a pretty story.

Was the Picayune *a good newspaper in its early days?*

Well . . . I'll tell you . . . if you'll turn that
thing off.

End of interview.

After Qwilleran snapped off the tape recorder,
Mrs. Gage said, "I can speak to you confidentially
because you're a friend of my favorite grandson.
Junior speaks highly of you. The truth is: I have
never thought well of that branch of the Goodwinter family, nor of the newspaper they published.
Ephraim, the founder of the *Picayune*, was not a
journalist. He was a rich mine owner and lumber
baron who would do anything for money. It was his
avarice and negligence that caused the terrible mine
explosion, killing thirty-nine men. Eventually he
took his own life. His sons were no better. His
grandson, Senior, was a strange one; he was interested only in *setting type*!" She rolled her eyes in de-
rision.

"Why did your daughter marry him?" Qwilleran
asked bluntly, since Euphonia was noted for blunt
candor.

"Gritty had *always* wanted to marry a Goodwinter, and she *always* did exactly what she wanted.
It was a strange match. She's a spirited girl who
likes a good time. Senior had no spirit at all and
was certainly not my idea of a good time. How they
produced Junior, I can't explain. He's too small to
be Gritty's offspring—she's such an amazon!—and
too smart to be Senior's son."

"Recessive genes," Qwilleran said. "He resembles his grandmother."

"You are a charming man, Mr. Qwilleran. I wish Junior might have had you for a father."

"You are a charming woman, Mrs. Gage."

They both paused for a moment of mutual admiration, and he found himself wishing she were thirty years younger. Spirit—that's what she had—spirit! Probably the result of all that *breathing*.

"Do you think Junior shows promise?" she asked.

"Great promise, Mrs. Gage. You can be proud of him. Were you aware that the *Picayune* was failing?"

"Of course I was aware. I tried to help. I don't know what the man did with my money, unless . . ."

"Unless what, Mrs. Gage?"

"I'll be perfectly frank. Let it all hang out, as Junior says. You see, I learned in a roundabout way that Senior had been making frequent one-day trips Down Below. To Minneapolis, as a matter of fact. If my son-in-law had ever shown any *spirit*, I would have guessed it was another woman. Under the circumstances, I could only deduce that he was gambling as a last resort—gambling and losing."

"Has it occurred to you that his death may have been suicide?"

She looked startled. "Senior would not have the spirit, Mr. Qwilleran, to take his own life."

Upon leaving, he said, "You are an excellent subject for an interview, Mrs. Gage. I hope we can meet again—perhaps for dinner some evening."

"I shall be delighted to accept if the invitation is still good in the spring. I leave for Florida tomorrow," she said. "This has been *such* a pleasure, Mr. Qwilleran. Now don't forget to *breathe*!"

Qwilleran was in a good mood that evening as he lounged in his favorite leather chair in the library, stroking the cat on his lap and waiting for a book to hit the carpet. He had stopped remonstrating; the book trick was becoming a game that he and Koko played together. The cat pulled out a title; Qwilleran read aloud, accompanied by purrs, iks, and yows.

On this occasion Koko's selection was *The Life of Henry V*, a good choice, Qwilleran thought. He thumbed through the pages for a passage he liked: the king's pep talk to his troops. *"Once more unto the breach, dear friend; once more!"*

Koko assumed his listening position, sitting tall and attentive on the desktop, his tail curled around his front paws, his blue eyes sparkling black in the lamplight.

It was a powerful speech, filled with graphic detail. *"But when the blast of war blows in our ears, then imitate the action of the tiger!"*

"Yow!" said Koko.

With such an appreciative audience Qwilleran was not shy about dramatizing the script. With a terrible look in his eyes he wrinkled his brow, stiffened his sinews, bared his teeth, stretched his nostrils, and breathed hard. Koko was purring hoarsely.

Bellowing at full volume, Qwilleran delivered the last line: *"Cry God for Harry! England and Saint George!"*

"YOW-OW!" Koko howled. Yum Yum fled from the room in alarm, and Mrs. Cobb came running.

"Oh! I thought you were being murdered, Mr. Q."

"Merely reading to Koko," he explained. "He seems to enjoy the sound of the human voice."

"It's *your* voice he likes. Last night everyone was saying you should join the theater group," she said.

When the household returned to its normal calm, a name flashed across Qwilleran's mind—Harry Noyton. He had had dealings with Harry Down Below. The man was a reckless entrepreneur who was always searching for a new challenge or a financial gamble. No matter how absurd the proposition, Harry always made it pay. He was currently living alone in Chicago, in a penthouse atop an office tower he had built.

On an impulse Qwilleran dialed Noyton's apartment, and a subhuman voice stated that he could be reached at his London hotel.

"How's that for a coincidence?" Quilleran asked Koko. "Harry's in England!" He glanced at his watch. Ten-thirty. It would be the middle of the night in London. All the better! Noyton had often roused him from sleep at an unearthly hour, and without apology.

He dialed the London hotel, expecting it to be

the Saint George, but it was Claridge's. When Noyton's voice came on the phone he sounded as vigorous as he did at high noon; his energy was phenomenal.

"Qwill! How's the boy? I hear you're living high on the hog since leaving the *Flux*. What's cookin'? I know you never spend a quarter on a phone call unless it's urgent."

"How would you like to be a newspaper tycoon, Harry?"

"Is the *Fluxion* up for sale?"

Qwilleran described the situation in Pickax, adding, "It would be a crime to prostitute a century-old newspaper as an advertising throwaway. The county needs a paper, and the *Picayune* name is part of everyone's life. It's had national publicity this week, and there's more to come. If someone made the widow a better offer, she might see the light."

"Hell, I'll talk to the widow. I'm good at talking to widows."

Qwilleran believed it. Noyton was a self-made man with a talent for attracting women as well as money, although he had never acquired any polish. Even in a tailor-made three-piece suit he succeeded in looking like a scarecrow. He had several ex-wives and was always looking for another.

"I'm flying home tomorrow," he said. "How do I get to Pickax? Never heard of the place."

"You fly to Minneapolis and then pick up a

hedgehopper to Moose County. Sorry I don't know the schedule. Probably they've never had one."

"I'll charter something. I'll get there somehow. Nobody can keep me on the ground for long."

"Better get here before snow flies."

"I'll give you a ring from Minneapolis."

"Good! I'll pick you up at the airport, Harry."

With a comfortable feeling of accomplishment, Qwilleran began his nightly house check and, in so doing, found another pigskin book on the floor. This time it was *All's Well That Ends Well.*

"It hasn't ended yet, old boy," he told Koko as he dropped the two protesting cats into the wicker hamper.

He was right. At two o'clock in the morning he was roused from sleep by a telephone call from Jody.

"Mr. Qwilleran, I'm so worried. Juney hasn't come home."

"Maybe he went to his mother's house. Have you called there?"

"There was no answer. Pug has gone back to Montana, and Mrs. Goodwinter is probably staying . . . in Indian Village. I called Grandma Gage earlier, and she thought Juney was still Down Below. I even called Roger, his friend in Mooseville."

"Then we'd better notify the police. I'll call the sheriff. You sit tight."

"I'm going crazy, Mr. Qwilleran. I feel like going out and looking for him myself."

"You can't do that, Jody. You should call a friend and have her stay with you. How about Francesca?"

"I hate to call her so late."

"I'll call her for you. A police chief's daughter is used to emergencies. Now you hang up so I can call the sheriff. And drink some warm milk, Jody."

SEVEN

Saturday, November sixteenth. "Possibility of snow squalls today with falling temperatures. Presently it's twenty-five degrees. Last night's low, fifteen. . . . And now for the news: A hunter reported missing early this morning has been found by sheriff's deputies aided by state troopers. Junior Goodwinter is listed in fair condition at Pickax Hospital, suffering from exposure and a broken leg."

As Qwilleran later learned from police chief Brodie, a deputy on routine patrol of side roads on the opening day of hunting season had spotted the red Jaguar parked near a wooded area. When Junior was reported missing, they were able to start the search at that point, using tracking dogs and the mounted posse, a volunteer group of farmers who were expert horsemen.

"It seems to me," Qwilleran said to Mrs. Cobb at the breakfast table, "that no one should go hunting alone. Too many hazards."

"Herb always goes alone," she said.

Qwilleran thought, That guy can't find anyone to go with him. Uncharitable thoughts came to his mind whenever Hackpole was mentioned. Aloud he said, "If he's taking you to dinner tonight, why not bring him in for a drink before you leave?"

"That would be nice," she said. "We'll have it right here in the kitchen. He'll be more comfortable here."

"Would he like a tour of the museum?"

"Well, to tell the truth, Mr. Q, he thinks art objects are dust catchers, but I'd like to show him the basement."

"You've never told me anything about his background," Qwilleran said, although he had heard about it from Junior.

"He grew up here. After a hitch in the army he worked on the East Coast, married, and had a couple of kids. They're grown-up now, and he doesn't even know where they are."

That fits the picture, Qwilleran thought.

"He came back to Moose County because of his wife's allergies, but she didn't like country life and she left him."

Ran off with a beer truck driver, Qwilleran had heard.

"He's a very lonely man, and I feel sorry for him."

"Has he shown you the farmhouse?"

"Not yet, but I know what I want to do—strip the wallpaper, paint the walls white, and stencil them."

"Would you like to have the big pine wardrobe? If so, it's your wedding present."

She gasped. "You mean the Pennsylvania German *schrank*? Oh, I'd love it! But are you sure you want to part with it?"

"My life will never be the same without it," he said. "I expect to have anxiety attacks and periods of great depression, and I may have to go into therapy, but I want you to have the *schrank*."

"Oh, Mr Q, you're kidding me again."

"Have you set a date?"

"Next Saturday if it's all right with you. Herb just wanted us to go to the courthouse, but I told him I wanted to be married here. Susan Exbridge is standing up for me. Would you be willing to be best man?"

He controlled a gulp. "Be glad to, Mrs. Cobb. Do you have a guest list? We'll have a champagne reception."

"That's very kind of you, but I don't think Herb would care for a reception, Mr. Q."

"Let me know if you change your mind. I want you to have a memorable wedding. You've been a valuable asset here."

"There's one favor I'd like to ask, if you don't mind," she said. "Would you speak to Koko about the herb garden? He keeps moving it around."

"Did you ever try speaking to a cat about *anything*?" Qwilleran asked. "He crosses his eyes and scratches his ear and goes right on doing what he was doing."

"I wouldn't mention it, but . . . after I've moved the garden into a sunny spot, he moves it into a dark corner. I've seen him do it. He stands on his hind legs, puts his paws on the lower shelf, and pushes."

The corners of Qwilleran's mouth twitched as he pictured Koko wheeling the herbs across the stone floor of the solarium like a baby carriage. Sunlight was not plentiful in November, and that cat wanted the best patches of sun for himself.

"Why don't you ask Hackpole to devise some kind of brake for the wheels?" he suggested.

The doorbell rang.

"Oh dear! I forgot to tell you," Mrs. Cobb said. "I guess I'm all discombobulated. Hixie Rice is stopping on her way to work. That's probably her at the front door." She jumped up.

"Sit still. I'll get it."

Hixie had parked her little car in the circular drive, and she was ogling the front door with its quantity of brass fittings polished to a dazzling brilliance by Mr. O'Dell.

"Everything is so grand, Qwill! You should have a butler," she said as her heels clicked across the white marble vestibule. "Here, I've brought you the latest delicacy in our frozen catfood line: lobster nuggets in Nantua sauce with anchovy garnish."

Koko made an immediately appearance in the foyer and stood staring at Hixie without expression, except for a fish-hook curve in his tail.

"I think he remembers me," Hixie said. *"Comment ça va, Monsieur Koko?"*

"Eeque, eeque," he replied. As Qwilleran gave Hixie a tour of the house, Koko followed like an overzealous security guard.

"Gorgeous rugs!" she said as they entered the drawing room.

The two large antique Aubussons were creamy in color, with borders and center medallions of faded pink roses.

"Watch Koko," Qwilleran said. "He always avoids stepping on the rose pattern."

"Weren't the old red dyes made from some kind of bug? Maybe he can smell it."

"After a hundred years? Don't try to explain it, Hixie. How about a cup of coffee?"

When they were settled comfortably in the library she gazed at the four thousand leather-bound books. "Did you find it traumatic, Qwill, to inherit a lot of money? Do you feel vulnerable or isolated or guilty?"

"Not particularly."

"Don't you find people envious or resentful or hostile?"

"You've been reading a book, Hixie. Actually, it's

just a nuisance to have a lot of money, so I turn it over to a philanthropic trust, and they get rid of it quietly."

She started to light a cigarette, and he stopped her. "City ordinance. No smoking in museums. . . . How's your friend's mother?"

"Who?"

"You said Tony's mother had a stroke and he had to fly to Philadelphia."

"Oh, she's getting better, and he's back here, working on his cookbook," Hixie said airily. "I'm going to write a book myself, on the rest rooms in country restaurants. They're not to be believed!"

"Don't complain. You're lucky the facilities are indoors. What's your objection?"

"Well, let me tell you about the North Pole Cafe in Brrr. They have only one rest room, and you have to dodge a very busy cook and a three-hundred-pound female dishwasher to get there. When I found it, between a garbage can and a sour mop, the room was dark, and I couldn't find the light switch. So the cook came and pulled a greasy string hanging from the ceiling, and *voilà*! the rest room was flooded with light from a fifteen-watt bulb.

"My next problem: how to close the door. It was wide open—and apparently stuck. When I tried forcing it, a toilet brush and a bleach bottle fell down on my head. You see, they kept the door open by hooking it to a high shelf where they kept the cleaning stuff. I got the thing closed and started groping for the john. I could hear a gurgling sound underfoot, from some kind of drain in the floor. Every once in a while it choked and gurgled and bubbled. I worried about that.

"The john seat was anchored by one bolt, and it was riding sort of sidesaddle. The floor drain kept gurgling and bubbling. The rusty washbowl started gasping and erupting, so I got out of there fast and made a bush stop on the way home."

"Hixie, you always exaggerate," Qwilleran said. "How was the food?"

"Fabulous! I mean it! And now there's something I'd like to discuss with you. Would Koko endorse our line of frozen catfoods? We'd design a 'Koko's Choice' label and have Koko T-shirts and other premiums. Maybe free bumper stickers saying, 'My Cat Loves Koko.' How does that go down?"

"I don't think he'd take kindly to exploitation. He doesn't go for anything unless it's his own idea."

"He could do TV commercials," she persisted. "Next week I'll bring a video camera and give him a screen test."

"That I've got to see," Qwilleran said. "How's everything at the Old Stone Mill?"

"My boss came in to dinner last night and said he's rewriting our contract, giving us a better deal."

"Congratulations!"

"He was feeling pretty good. He had some woman with him—not his wife—and they went through two bottles of our best champagne."

"I hear his divorce is now final."

"He's not wasting any time. The two of them

were planning a southern cruise and hoping they could get away before snow flies."

"What did she look like?" Qwilleran asked.

"The hearty athletic type with a loud laugh—the kind I can't stand! Mr. X has an apartment in our complex, and I think she's moved in. Why is everyone around here so concerned about snow flying?"

Snow did not fly on Saturday, although it was still being predicted on the hourly weathercasts. Qwilleran was listening to the six o'clock news in the library when Mrs. Cobb peeked into the room.

"He's here," she said nervously.

Qwilleran followed her to the kitchen to greet the man who was stealing his housekeeper. He gave Hackpole a handshake intended to be hearty and sincere and found his fingers crushed in a powerful grip.

"They say we can expect some snow tonight," Qwilleran said, employing Moose County's standard conversation opener.

"It won't snow for a few days yet," Hackpole said. "I've been out in the woods all day, and I can tell by the way the whitetails are acting."

"I hear you're an expert woodsman, and I'd like to hear more about that, but first . . . how about a drink? Mrs. Cobb, what is your pleasure?"

"Do you think I could have a whiskey sour?" she asked coyly.

"Shot and a beer for me," her date said. He was wearing his date-night attire: a corduroy sports coat with plaid flannel shirt. Koko had been circling him and finally ventured to sniff his shoes.

"Scat!" yelled Hackpole, stamping his foot.

Koko did not even blink.

"What's the matter with that cat? Is it deaf?" he asked. "I can make most cats jump two feet off the floor."

"Koko considers himself licensed to sniff shoes," Qwilleran said. "He knows you have dogs at home."

The three of them pulled up chairs around the ancient kitchen table imported from a Spanish monastery.

"Looks like you could use a new table," said the guest, surveying three centuries of carefully preserved distress marks. He tossed off the shot and then poked three fingers in the breast pocket of his sports coat.

Mrs. Cobb tapped his hand in an affectionate rebuke. "No smoking, dear. It's bad for the antiques, and it's forbidden by law in museums."

He left the cigarettes in his pocket and looked warily at Koko. "Why does it sit there staring at me?" he demanded with the irritability of a smoker who has been told not to smoke.

"Koko is evaluating you," Qwilleran said. "The data will be programmed in the minicomputer in his brain."

"We always used to have a pack of barn cats around," said the guest. "We'd tie a tin can to a

cat's tail and have a swell moving target for a .22."
He laughed, but he was the only one who did.

Qwilleran said, "If you tied a can to Koko's tail,
he'd sit and stare at a point between your eyes until
you began to feel dizzy. Soon there would be a dull
ache under your left shoulder blade, then a stabbing
abdominal pain. Your feet would get numb, and
you'd find it hard to breathe. Then your blood
would start to itch. Do you know what it feels like
to have itching blood?"

Mrs. Cobb patted her friend's hand. "He's only
kidding, dear. He's always kidding." She saw him
fingering the cigarette pack again. "Oops! Musn't
do!"

Hackpole threw the pack on the table.

"I hear you're pretty good with a deer rifle,"
Qwilleran said amiably.

"Yeah, I'm a pretty good shooter. I've hunted elk,
moose, grizzlies—everything. The whitetail's my favorite, though. I've got some eight-point trophy
bucks mounted, but the forkhorn gives the best
meat. That's what I brought in yesterday. I always
get my buck the first day."

Qwilleran thought, I'll bet he does some poaching
the rest of the year.

"I made a clean kill and made sure it was well
bled out. Then I gutted it, slung it over my back,
and carried it to my pickup. I was home by noon. It
weighed in at one ninety-eight."

Qwilleran mentally subtracted fifty pounds.

With a hint of pride Mrs. Cobb said, "Herb is a still-hunter."

"Yeah. You don't know about still-hunting, I bet."

Qwilleran had to admit his ignorance.

"Still-hunters, we don't sit behind a bush and wait for something to come down the trail. You hafta move around, looking for game—very slow, very careful, very quiet. When you sight your buck, you stalk it and wait for the best shot. You hafta move like a deer and make noise like a deer would. Like, no zippers, no cigarette lighters. You hafta have good eyes and a good running shot. Lotta satisfaction in still-hunting."

"I'm impressed," Qwilleran said as he poured another shot for his guest. "I understand you're also a volunteer fire fighter."

"I'm quittin'," Hackpole said, looking disgruntled. "A lotta women are joining up. I don't mind them running a canteen when it's an all-night fire, but they got no business driving a truck and hanging around the fire hall."

The bride-to-be said, "I'm glad he's giving it up. It's terribly dangerous."

"Yeah, smoke inhalation, for one thing. Or you're trying to vent a fire and the roof caves in. Once I saw a hose get away from the nozzleman and go whipping around, cracking heads and breaking bones. You don't know the power of water going through a hose! There's a lotta stuff people don't know."

"I've always wondered why firemen go crazy with the ax," Qwilleran said.

"We gotta vent the fire, so the smoke and heat can get out and we can go into the building and knock down the blaze."

"Any idea what caused the *Picayune* fire?"

"Started in the basement. That's all anybody knows. My shop did some repair work on those old presses. They had a drip pan underneath to catch the solvent when they cleaned off the ink. There was a lotta rags, a lotta paper. Bad business! The stairs acted like a flue, and the fire went right up to the roof."

"Well, dear," Mrs. Cobb said, "we ought to be going, but first I want you to see the pub in the basement."

The original builders of the mansion had imported an English pub from London, complete with bar, tavern tables and chairs, even wall paneling.

It was something Hackpole could appreciate. "Hey, you could get a liquor license and open a tavern down here," he said.

As they rode the elevator back to the main floor, Qwilleran asked where they were going to dinner.

"Otto's Tasty Eats. One price—all you can eat." He fingered his breast pocket. "Where's my cigarettes?"

"You left them on the kitchen table, dear," said Mrs. Cobb.

"I don't see the damn things," he called from the kitchen.

"Did you look in all your pockets?"

"It don't matter. I got another pack in the glove compartment."

Qwilleran extended his hand. "I'm glad we could finally meet, and let me congratulate you on finding a wonderful—"

He was interrupted by a loud crash. It came from the rear of the house. He and the housekeeper rushed into the solarium, followed slowly by their guest. The place was in darkness, but a pale, ghostly shape streaked out of the room as they entered.

When the lights were switched on, the catastrophe was revealed. In the middle of the floor stood the mobile herb garden, and nearby was a clay pot, smashed, with soil and foliage scattered in every direction. Other plants had been uprooted from their pots and flung about the room, and the floor was a gritty mess of soil and leaves.

"Oh dear! Oh dear!" said Mrs. Cobb in shock and dismay.

"It's our resident ghost," Qwilleran explained to Hackpole. "Did Mrs. Cobb tell you we have a ghost?"

Nobly she said, "Every old house should have a ghost," but there was a tremor in her voice, and she glanced around uneasily for a glimpse of the guilty cat.

"We'll replace everything," Qwilleran reassured her. "Don't worry. You two go to dinner, and I'll clean up the mess. Have a nice evening."

As soon as the couple had left, he went in search

of the Siamese. As he expected, they were in the library, looking innocent and satisfied. He stepped on a small bump and found a cigarette under the Bokhara rug. That was Yum Yum's contribution to the occasion. Koko had his chin on his paw and his paw on the cover of a pigskin-bound book. He raised his head and turned bright expectant eyes on the man.

"I'm not going to read to you. You don't deserve it," Qwilleran said quietly but firmly. "That was a wicked thing to do. You know how much Mrs. Cobb loves her herb garden, and our food tastes better because of the things she grows. So don't expect any kind words from me! You lie there and contemplate your sins, and try to be a better cat in the future. . . . I'm going out to dinner."

He wrested the book away from Koko. It was *Hamlet* again. Before returning it to the shelf he sniffed it. Qwilleran had a keen sense of smell, but all he could detect was the odor of *old book*. He sniffed *Macbeth* and the other titles Koko had dislodged. They all smelled like *old book*. Then he compared the odor with titles that Koko had so far ignored: *Othello*, *As You Like It*, and *Antony and Cleopatra*. He had to admit they all smelled exactly the same—like *old book*. He went out to dinner.

EIGHT

Sunday, November seventeeth. "Light snow turning to freezing rain," was the prediction. Actually, the sun was shining, and Qwilleran looked forward to taking a long walk.

Over the breakfast pancakes he apologized profusely to the housekeeper. "I'm really sorry about your herb garden, Mrs. Cobb. The pot he broke contained mint, which is related to catnip, I believe. Why he uprooted the others is a mystery. We'll replace them all."

"It won't be that easy," she said. "Four of them were started from seed in a cold frame at Herb's place. The others were plants, and we can't buy them at this time of year."

"There was no point in scolding him. Unless you catch a cat in the act and rap him on the nose, he doesn't connect the reprimand with the misdemeanor. That's what Lori Bamba said, and she knows all about cats. No doubt it was Yum Yum who stole the cigarettes. I found one under a rug and another behind a seat cushion."

"And I found the empty pack under a rug in the upstairs hall," Mrs. Cobb said.

"I'm afraid your evening got off to a bad start. Did you enjoy dinner?"

She pursed her lips, then admitted, "Well, we had a little argument. When he found out that cigarette smoke is injurious to antiques, he said I can't use them in the farmhouse. He's practically a chain-smoker."

"Could you use reproductions?"

"I hate copies, Mr. Q. I've lived too long with the real thing."

"There must be some compromise."

"I can think of one good compromise," she said crisply. "He can give up his smelly habit. You don't hear the surgeon general issuing any warnings against *antiques*!"

Qwilleran made sympathetic noises, then excused himself, saying he wanted to go out and buy a Sunday *Fluxion*.

He walked with a light step for two reasons. He sensed a rift between Mrs. Cobb and Hackpole that might forestall the marriage. And . . . he had received an invitation from Polly Duncan.

"Thursday is my day off," she had said. "Why don't you drive out to my cottage, and I'll do a roast with Yorkshire pudding? Come before dark; the house is easier to find in daylight."

He walked briskly. It was four miles around the periphery of Pickax, and on the way he met the fire chief, going into the drugstore for the Sunday *Fluxion*.

Qwilleran said, "Where's the snow that Moose County is famous for?"

"Couldna say, but this weather will do till the white stuff comes along."

"Explain something to me, Scottie. Pickax has a strange arrangement of streets. Nothing makes sense."

"It were laid out by two miners and a lumberjack on payday," said Scottie, "or so the story goes."

"How do the fire trucks ever find the right address? The city's bounded on the south by South Street—nothing wrong with that—but it's bounded on the north by East Street, on the west by North Street, and on the east by West Street. The ball field is at the corner of South North Street and West South Street. It could drive a logical mind crazy."

"Dunna look for logic up here, laddie," said Scottie, shaking his shaggy gray head.

"Did the fire marshal fly up to investigate the *Picayune* fire?"

"We needna call him unless it looks like arson, or somebody dies in the fire. And this one, it were accidental combustion caused by oily rags and solvents in the pressroom."

"How can you tell when a fire has been set?"

"Are you plannin' a little arson, laddie?"

"Not in the foreseeable future, Scottie."

"Weel, if you do, avoid leavin' a two-gallon jerry can on the premises, painted red and smellin' like gasoline. And dunna throw the match too soon. The explosion can throw you out the door."

"Can you tell when the fire starts with an explosion?"

"Aye. If the door is blown off the hinges—that's one way. And if the walls are charred deep."

Qwilleran finished his walk, stopping for a cup of coffee at a diner on N. North Street and the Sunday paper at a party store on S. West Street.

In the afternoon, as he was reading the *Fluxion* and counting typographical errors, the doorbell rang, and when he went to the front entrance he found an elderly face peering from the hood of a parka.

"Good afternoon," said the caller in a cheerful high-pitched voice. "Do you have any mouseholes you want plugged?"

"I beg your pardon?"

"Mouseholes. I'm good at plugging mouseholes."

Qwilleran was puzzled. Workmen always came to

the service entrance; they never came on Sunday; and they were usually much younger.

"I was just taking my constitutional," said the old man. "It's a nice day for a walk. I'm Homer Tibbitt from the Old Timers Club."

"Of course! I didn't recognize you in the parka. Come in!"

"I saw your cat parading around with a mouse at the party, and I thought you might have some mouseholes you want plugged. I'd do it gratis."

"Let me take your coat, and we'll sit down and talk about it. Would you like a cup of coffee?"

"I'll take some if it's decaffeinated, and it won't hurt if you put a drop of brandy in it to start the old furnace working again."

They went into the library, Mr. Tibbitt walking vigorously with arms and legs flailing in awkward coordination. There was a fire in the grate, and he stood with his back to the warmth. "I'm used to old houses like this," he said. "I was volunteer custodian at the Lockmaster Museum in the county below. Have you heard of it?"

"Can't say that I have. I'm new up here."

"It was a shipbuilder's mansion—all wood construction—and I plugged fifty-seven mouseholes. In a stone house like this the mice have to be smarter, but we have smart mice in Pickax."

"What brought you up here to the Snow Belt, Mr. Tibbitt?"

"I was born here, and the old homestead was standing empty. There was another reason, too; a retired English teacher down in Lockmaster was chasing me. They like retired principals. I was principal of Pickax Upper School when I retired. I'm ninety-three. I started teaching school seventy years ago."

"You should have brought your English teacher to Pickax," Qwilleran said. "I've never heard so many butchered verbs and pronouns."

The principal gave an angular gesture of despair. "We've always tried our best, but there's a saying up here—if you'll pardon the grammar: Country folks is different, and Moose County folks is more different."

Despite his creaking joints, the old man was enormously energetic, and Qwilleran said, "Retirement seems to agree with you, Mr. Tibbitt."

"Keep busy! That's the ticket! Now, if you want me to do a survey on the mousehole situation . . ."

Qwilleran hesitated. "We have a janitor, you know. . . ."

"I've known Pat O'Dell since he was in the first grade. He's a good boy, but he hasn't made a study of mouseholes."

"Before we launch a campaign against *mus musculus*, Mr. Tibbitt, I'd like to get some of your recollections on tape for the oral history program—that is, if you would be willing."

"Turn on the machine. Ask me some questions. Just give me another cup of coffee with a drop of brandy—make it two drops—and be sure it's decaffeinated."

The following interview with Homer Tibbitt was later transcribed:

Question: What can you tell us about the early schools in Moose County?

Beginning way back when my mother was a schoolmarm, they were built of logs—just one room with desks around the walls, hard benches with no backs, and a potbellied stove in the middle. And they were drafty! She taught in one school where the snow blew through the chinks, and there were rabbit tracks in the snow on the floor.

What was required of a teacher in those days?

My mother walked three miles to school and got there early enough to sweep the floor and start a wood fire in the stove. She taught eight grades in one room—without any textbooks! Her pay was a dollar a day plus free board and room with a farm family. Male teachers were paid two dollars.

How many students did she have in that one room?

Thirty or forty enrolled, but only half of them ever showed up for classes.

What subjects did she teach?

She was supposed to teach the three Rs, history, geography, grammar, penmanship, and orthography. She also organized games and special programs, and she was required to lecture on the evils of drink, tobacco, and tight corsets.

How about team sports? Was there athletic competition?

They played games at recess, and there was rivalry between schools, but it was over spelling matches, not football.

Had conditions improved when you started to teach?

We still had one-room schools, but they were well built, and we had textbooks. We still didn't have indoor plumbing. . . . Could I bother you for another cup of coffee? My mouth gets dry.

Did you know any of the Goodwinters connected with the newspaper?

I retired before Junior was born, but I had his father in my classes. Senior was a quiet boy with a one-track mind. I grew up with Titus and Samson, and I knew the old man. When I was eleven years old I worked as a printer's devil after school. Ephraim Goodwinter made plenty of money in mining, but he was greedy. Ever hear about the explosion that killed thirty-two men? The engineers had warned Ephraim, but he wouldn't spend the money on safety measures. After the explosion he tried to make it right by donating a public library.

Is it true he hanged himself?

Aha! That's one of Moose County's dirty little secrets. The family said it was suicide, and the coroner said it was suicide, but everybody knew he was *lynched*, and everybody knew who was in the lynching party. The whole town turned out for his funeral. They wanted to be sure he didn't come back, the saying was.

What happened to Titus and Samson?

There was a cock-and-bull story about Samson's horse being frightened by a flock of blackbirds and that's how he was killed. Then Titus was murdered by the *Picayune* wagon driver. Died with his derby hat on his head.

Who was the wagon driver?

Zack Whittlestaff. This county is full of curious names: Cuttlebrink, Dingleberry, Fitzbottom—almost Elizabethan. I used to have a Falstaff in one of my classes, and a Scroop. Straight out of Shakespeare, eh?

Would you say there was a vendetta against the Goodwinters?

Well, the relatives of the explosion victims hated Ephraim, you can be sure of that. Zack was one of them. He was a ruffian. No good in school. Married a Scroop girl. I had their two children in my classes. The girl got into trouble and drowned herself. Left a suicide note addressed to her cat—probably the only living being that loved the poor girl.

End of interview.

The recording session was interrupted by a phone call from Minneapolis. Harry Noyton was on his way. His chartered plane would arrive at the Pickax airport at five-thirty.

"How's the weather up there?" Noyton asked.

"No snow, but it's cold. I hope you're bringing warm clothing."

"Hell, I don't own any warm clothes. I grab a heated taxi when I want to go somewhere."

"There are no taxis in Moose County," Qwilleran said. "We'll have to buy you some long johns and a hat with earflaps. Meet you at five-thirty."

He allowed plenty of time for driving. Airport Road ran through deer country. At dusk they would be feeding and moving around. Gun hunters had been in the woods for three days, stirring them up and making them nervous. Qwilleran drove cautiously.

While waiting for the plane to land he had a few words with Charlie. "Do you think we'll get any snow this winter?"

"It's kinda late, but when it comes it'll be the Big One."

"I hear you've lost a good customer."

"Who?"

"Senior Goodwinter."

"Yeah. Too bad. He was a nice fellah. Killed himself with work. Most people are always taking off for Florida or Vegas or somewhere, but all he ever did was fly down to Minneapolis on business and come back the same day. That's why I say he killed himself with work. Fell asleep at the wheel, most likely."

When Noyton galumphed off the plane, he had a light raincoat flapping around his lanky figure, and he carried a traveling bag just large enough for a razor and an extra shirt. That was his style. He boasted he could fly around the world with a toothbrush and a credit card.

"Qwill, you old rooster! You look like a farmer with those boots and that hat!"

"And you look like a visitor from outer space," Qwilleran said. "You'll frighten the natives with that three-piece suit. First thing tomorrow we'll take you to Scottie's Men's Shop and buy some camouflage. . . . Buckle up, Harry," he added as he turned on the ignition in his small car.

"Hell, I never fastened a seat belt in my life, except on planes."

Qwilleran turned off the ignition and folded his arms. "There are ten thousand deer in Moose County, Harry. This is the rutting season. At this time of evening all the bucks chase all the does back and forth across the highway. If we hit a buck, you'll go through the windshield, so buckle up."

"Jeez! The odds are better at the Beirut airport!"

"Last winter a buck chased a doe down Main Street in Pickax, and they both went through the plate-glass window of a furniture store. Landed in a water bed."

Noyton fastened his seat belt and stared anxiously at the road for the next ten miles, while

Qwilleran scanned the cornfields and thickets for movement.

"If we encounter a buck, Harry, do you want me to hit him broadside and risk having his hooves come through the windshield, or shall I try to avoid him and land upside down in a ditch?"

"Jeez! Do I have a choice?" said Noyton, gripping the dashboard with both hands.

When they reached the outskirts of Pickax, Qwilleran said, "Here's the program. Tomorrow I turn you over to the mayor and the economic development people. He'll put you in touch with the widow—and she's a merry one, I might add. Tonight I'll take you to dinner at the Old Stone Mill. After that there's a bedroom suite awaiting you at the palace I inherited. You have your choice of Old English with side curtains on the bed, or Biedermeier with flowers painted on everything, or Empire with enough sphinxes and gryphons to give you nightmares."

"To tell the truth, Qwill, I'd be a helluva lot more comfortable in a hotel. It gives me more flexibility. I had a meal in Minneapolis, and now I'd like to turn in. Any objection?"

"None at all. The New Pickax Hotel is centrally located near the city hall."

"Building new hotels, are they?" Noyton said with obvious approval.

"The New Pickax Hotel was built in 1935 after the original hotel burned down. It has a part-time bellhop, color TV in the lobby, indoor plumbing, and locks on the doors."

He dropped Noyton at the hotel entrance. "Call me tomorrow when you're rested, and I'll pick you up for breakfast. I want a private talk with you before turning you over to the mayor."

At the end of the day Qwilleran and his two friends relaxed in the library for a while before lights-out. Yum Yum sat on his lap with her back in a convenient position for stroking, and Koko sat tall and alert on the desktop, awaiting conversation.

Qwilleran began in an even, conciliatory tone. "I don't know what to say to you, Koko. You're not usually destructive—unless you have a reason. Why did you ruin the herb garden?"

The cat squeezed his eyes and made a small sound without opening his mouth.

"It won't do any good to act contrite. The damage is done. If you're trying to alienate our splendid housekeeper, you're cutting off your whiskers to spite your face. You won't eat half so well when she's married and living somewhere else."

Koko hopped from the desk to the bookshelf and started pawing at the set of plays.

"No readings tonight. I've had a full day. But we'll play Mr. Tibbitt's tape and see how it sounds."

The small portable recorder made the old man's high-pitched voice even more nasal and shrill, and Koko shook his head and batted his ears with a paw.

There was the ring of a telephone bell on the tape,

and the recording came to an abrupt end. Qwilleran stroked his moustache reflectively. "Ephraim was lynched," he said aloud. "Titus was knifed. The other brother—Samson—was probably ambushed. And Senior was . . . what? Was his death an accident? Or was it suicide? Or was it murder?"

"Yow!" said Koko, and Qwilleran felt a significant twinge in the roots of his moustache.

NINE

Monday, November eighteenth. "An unexpected cold snap brought temperatures as low as five degrees in Pickax last night, six below in Brrr, but a warming trend is indicated with a few snow flurries this afternoon."

Qwilleran snapped off his car radio with an impatient gesture. Despite the predictions, Moose County had yet to see even a light dusting of snow. He was driving to the New Pickax Hotel in the limousine that he had inherited from the Klingenschoen estate, the better to impress the visitor from Down Below.

When Noyton saw the long black vehicle, he said, "Jeez! Qwill, you've really got it made! How come? Did you marry oil? No one ever told me why you left the *Fluxion*. I thought you retired to write a book."

"It's a long story," Qwilleran said. "First I want to show you where I live and treat you to one of my housekeeper's memorable breakfasts."

"You—with a housekeeper as well as a limo? I remember when you lived in a furnished room and rode the bus."

"Actually I live over the garage, and I'm turning the house into a museum."

In a state of wonder Noyton walked into the K mansion and said, "I know kings in Europe that don't live this good. One thing I want to know: Why am I here? Why don't you finance this newspaper yourself?"

It was a question that Qwilleran was tired of hearing. He explained his position. "I'm a writer, Harry, not an entrepreneur." He related the history of the *Picayune* and reiterated the county's crying need for a newspaper.

"Who's going to run it?" was Noyton's first question.

"Arch Riker has just left the *Fluxion*. He's a great editor and knows the business inside out. Junior Goodwinter is the last of a long line of newspaper Goodwinters. He's a trained journalist. His academic record is tops, and he has boundless energy and enthusiasm."

"Sounds like my kind of joe. Who's the widow?"

"Gritty Goodwinter . . ."

"I like her already!"

"She wants to sell the newspaper to a close personal friend who'll only exploit the name of the hundred-year-old publication. Of course, you could forget the *Picayune* and start something called the *Backwoods Gazette* or the *Moose Call*, but the *Picayune* had a million dollars' worth of publicity last week and is due for more in a national news magazine."

"I got the picture," Noyton said. "We'll get the paper away from those bastards."

"Mrs. Goodwinter also has a barnful of antique printing presses. You could start a newspaper museum."

"I like it!" Noyton exclaimed. "What made you think of me, anyway?"

Qwilleran hesitated. They were eating breakfast, and Koko was under the table hoping someone would drop a strip of bacon. "Well, it's like this: Your name just popped into my head." How could he explain to a man like Noyton that the cat had drawn his attention to a certain book? No, it was too farfetched.

After breakfast the two men paid a visit to Scottie's Men's Shop. The proprietor burred his *r*'s and sold Noyton a raccoon car coat, an Aussie hat, and some tooled leather boots. For the rest of the day the big ungainly man with a craggy face was highly visible in Pickax.

He was seen leaving the hotel, entering the city hall, driving around with the mayor, lunching with influential men at the country club, walking out of the law office, walking into the bank, dining with the Goodwinter widow, and eating a twenty-ounce steak with two baked potatoes.

It was rumored that he was a Texan buying oil rights that would make Moose County farmers rich. Or he was a speculator promoting offshore drilling that would ruin the tourist industry. Or he was the advance man for a nuclear power plant that would leak radiation, contaminate the drinking water, and kill the fish. Or he was a Hollywood scout for a major movie to be made in Moose County. The rumors were reported by Mrs. Cobb, who had heard them from Mrs. Fulgrove, who had been told by Mr. O'Dell.

Meanwhile Qwilleran made a morning visit to the hospital to see the young newspaper editor who was known for his boundless energy and enthusiasm. Junior was slumped in a chair with his leg in a cast, his face unshaven, and his expression disgruntled. Jody was flitting about, trying to be cheerful and useful, but Junior was being stubbornly morose.

"You idiot!" Qwilleran greeted the patient. "If you're going to break a leg, why not pick a more comfortable place?"

Jody said, "He caught a bad cold in the woods, but it didn't go into pneumonia. He wants to stay in the hospital until his beard grows."

"Nowhere else to go," Junior said hopelessly.

"The farmhouse is sold. The furniture is being auctioned off Wednesday. I can't stay with Jody; all she's got is a studio apartment."

"We have some spare beds you're welcome to use," Qwilleran said.

"I don't know. I just don't know what to do."

"Well, wipe that bleak look off your face. I have some good news. An acquaintance of mine from Down Below wants to buy a newspaper. He's prepared to offer your mother three times what XYZ has offered, and he'll sink a bundle into a new printing plant."

Junior looked wary. "Is he crazy?"

"Crazy and loaded. He owns office buildings, hotels, ball clubs, a chain of restaurants, and a couple of breweries in the U.S. and abroad, and he likes the idea of owning a newspaper. He might get into magazines later on."

"I don't believe it. I'm hallucinating. Or you're hallucinating."

Jody cried, "Oh, Juney! Isn't that fabulous?"

Qwilleran went on. "Noyton is here now. The city fathers are gung ho. The plan is for Arch Riker to be the publisher, and you'll be managing editor of a real newspaper. I know some young journalists Down Below who are disenchanted with the city, and they'll find this a good place to raise a family. They won't earn as much as they did Down Below, but it costs less to live up here. Who knows? We might get Noyton to finance a decent airport and buy an airline. We'll have to monitor his enthusiasm, though, or he'll build a fifty-story hotel in the middle of a corn-field."

Junior was speechless.

"Oh, Juney," his little friend kept squealing, "say something."

"Are you sure it's going through?"

"Noyton never backs down."

"But my mother has this . . . close connection with Exbridge."

"Connection! She's having an affair with Exbridge, and you know it. But if she's as hungry as it appears, she'll forget about XYZ and go for the larger fish. Not only will Noyton jingle hard cash in her ears; he'll turn on the charm. Women like him."

"Is he married?" asked Jody.

"Not at the moment, but he's too old for you, Jody."

She giggled.

"He's interested in buying the old presses in the barn also, to start a newspaper museum. Your father would be pleased, Junior."

"Oh, wow!"

"Jody," said Qwilleran, "would you get us some coffee from the cafeteria? And some of those oat-meal cookies made out of cardboard and sawdust?" He handed her a bill and waited for her to disappear. "Before she returns, Junior, answer a few questions, will you? Do you think your father's accident might have been suicide?"

Junior stared. "I don't think—he'd do—anything like that?"

"He had bankrupted the family. Your mother was having an affair. And there might be another reason."

"What do you mean?"

"Do you remember that stranger in a black raincoat who came up here on the plane? You thought he was a traveling salesman. I think he was an investigator of some kind. If your father was involved in anything shady, he might have known the man was coming. . . ."

"My dad wouldn't do anything illegal," Junior protested. "He didn't have that kind of mind."

"Next question: Could it have been murder?"

"WHAT!" Junior almost jumped out of his cast. "Why would . . . who would . . . ?"

"Skip that one. What was in the metal box you tried to save after the fire?"

"I don't know. Dad was very secretive about it, but I knew it was important."

"How big was it?"

Junior sneezed and reached for a tissue. "About as big as a tissue box."

"I hear Jody coming. Tell me this: Why was your father making frequent one-day trips to Minneapolis?"

"He never told me." Junior's face turned red. "But I know he wasn't getting along with my mother."

Jody returned with the coffee. "No oatmeal cookies left, so I brought molasses."

"They taste like burnt tires," Junior said after a

couple of nibbles. "How was the turnout at the pre-view, Qwill?"

"Full house! I've started interviewing the Old Timers and taping oral histories. Got any sugges-tions? I've got your grandmother and Homer Tibbitt on tape."

"Mrs. Woolsmith," Jody said in a small voice. "She'd be a good one."

Junior scratched his emerging beard. "You should be able to find some who remember the mines and the pioneer farms and the fishing industry before powerboats."

"Mrs. Woolsmith lived on a farm," Jody said softly.

"I need a subject with a reliable memory," Qwilleran said.

"You'll still have to drag it out of them," Junior warned him. "The Old Timers like to talk about their blood pressure and their dentures and their great-grandchildren."

Jody said, "Mrs. Woolsmith has almost all her own teeth."

"Well, give it some thought," Qwilleran said to Junior. "There's no hurry."

"Wait a minute! I've got it! There's a woman in the senior care facility," Junior suddenly recalled. "She's over ninety, but she's sharp, and she spent all her life on a farm. Her name is Woolsmith. Sarah Woolsmith."

Jody picked up her coat and shoulder bag and walked quietly from the room.

"Hey, where's she going?" Junior yelled.

Following his session at the hospital, Qwilleran went to lunch at Stephanie's, wondering about Senior's metal box and his frequent trips to Minneapolis. Junior's red-faced embarrassment meant that he knew or suspected the reason. Young people who are quite casual in their own relationships can be strangely embarrassed by the sexual adventures of their elders. As he was musing about this curious reaction, he heard a familiar voice at the table behind him.

A man was ordering a roast beef sandwich with mustard and horseradish. "Trim the fat, please. And bring a tossed salad with Roquefort dressing and no cucumber or green pepper."

The voice had a clipped twang that Qwilleran had heard before. He rose and walked in the direction of the men's room, glancing at his neighbor as he passed. It was the so-called historian he had confronted in the library. The man had exchanged his buttoned-down image for more casual attire—less conspicuous in Moose County—but there was no doubt about his identity. He was the stranger whose previous visit had coincided with Senior's fatal accident—or suicide—or murder.

Qwilleran spent the rest of his lunch hour sifting the possibilities. He composed scenarios involving the metal box . . . adultery . . . gambling . . . the drug connection . . . espionage. In none of them did the mild-mannered typesetter seem to fit.

TEN

Tuesday, November nineteenth. "Warmer today, with highs in the upper twenties. Some chance of snow this afternoon, with blizzard conditions developing Wednesday. Currently our temperature is nineteen."

"That's terrible!" Mrs. Cobb said. "Tomorrow's the auction, and it's way out in the country. They say the hotel's already full of out-of-town dealers. They came for the preview this afternoon."

"Don't worry. If they predict a blizzard, it'll be a nice day," Qwilleran said with the cynicism of a Moose County weather nut. "How will they handle an auction in a house like that? It's nothing but a series of small rooms."

"The actual auction will probably be in the barn. The posters and radio announcements said to dress warm. Foxy Fred is handling it, so everything will be done right. I'm going to the preview this afternoon to pick up a catalogue. What time is Miss Rice coming? The cats are hungry."

At Hixie's suggestion the Siamese had been given only a teaspoonful of food for breakfast—only enough to keep them from chewing ankles. The idea was that Koko should be ravenously hungry for this screen test, and Yum Yum had to suffer with him. They yowled constantly while Qwilleran ate his eggs Benedict. They paced the floor, got underfoot, and screeched when a foot accidentally came down upon a tail.

Koko evidently knew that Hixie was responsible for this outrage. Upon her arrival he greeted her with a button-eyed glare and a switching tail.

"*Bonjour, Monsieur Koko,*" she said. He turned and walked stiff-legged into the laundry room, where he scratched the gravel in his commode.

"Here's my scenario," she explained to Qwilleran. "We start with a shot of the front door, which denotes elegance and wealth at a glance. Then we enter the foyer, and the camera pans from the French furniture to the grand staircase to the crystal chandelier."

"It sounds like prime-time soap opera."

"Next we zoom to the top of the staircase, where Koko is sitting, looking bored."

"Who's going to direct this?" Qwilleran wanted to know.

Hixie ignored the question. "Then the butler announces in a starchy voice that pork liver cupcakes are served. That's voice-over. You can do the voice-over, Qwill. Immediately Koko runs downstairs, flowing in that liquid way he has, and the camera follows him into the dining room."

"Dining room?" Qwilleran muttered doubtfully. The Siamese were accustomed to meals in the kitchen and were reluctant to eat in the wrong location.

Hixie went on with her usual confidence. "Quick shot of the twenty-foot dining table with three-foot silver candelabra and a single elegant porcelain plate. We can use one of the Klingenschoen service plates with the blue border and gold crest and *K* monogram. . . . Then . . . cut to Koko devouring the pork liver cupcakes avidly. We may need to do several takes, so be prepared to grab him, Qwill. The trick is to avoid rear-end shots."

"That won't be easy. Cats are fond of mooning."

"Okay, you put him on the top stair."

Koko had been listening with an expression that could be described only as sour. When Qwilleran stooped to pick him up, he slipped from his grasp like a wet bar of soap, streaked down the foyer in a blur of movement, and sprang to the top of the Pennsylvania *schrank*. From this seven-foot perch he gazed down at his pursuers defiantly. He was sitting dangerously close to a large, rare majolica vase.

"I don't dare climb up and grab him," Qwilleran said. "He's taken a hostage. He probably knows it's worth ten thousand dollars."

"I didn't know he was so temperamental," Hixie said.

"Let's have a cup of coffee in the kitchen and see what happens when we ignore him. Siamese hate to be ignored."

In a few minutes Koko joined them, sauntering into the room with a swaggering show of nonchalance. He sat on his haunches like a kangaroo and innocently licked a small patch of fur on his underside. When this chore was finished he allowed himself to be carried to the top of the staircase.

Hixie directed from below. "Arrange him in a compact bundle on the top step, Qwill, facing the camera."

He lowered the cat gently to the carpeted stair, but Koko stiffened his body. His back humped, his tail curled into a corkscrew, and all four legs looked out-of-joint.

"Try it again," Hixie called up to them. "Tuck his legs under his body."

"You come up and tuck his legs under his body," Qwilleran said, "and I'll go down and take the pictures. Your scenario is good, Hixie, but it won't play."

"Well, bring him down, and we'll do a close-up with the catfood to see how he looks on camera."

Qwilleran lugged Koko into the dining room. By now the cat was a squirming, protesting, nasty, snarling bundle of flying fur.

"Ready, Mrs. Cobb!" Hixie shouted toward the kitchen.

The housekeeper, who was standing by as prop-person, trotted from the kitchen carrying a plate heaped with gray pork paste. "Is this going to be in color?" she asked.

Carefully Qwilleran placed Koko in front of the plate—profile to the camera—while Hixie moved in with her telephoto lens. Koko looked down at the gray blob, with his ears and whiskers swept backward in loathing. He picked up one fastidious paw and shook it in distaste. Then he shook the other paw and slowly walked away, switching his tail.

Qwilleran said, "If you ever need a picture of a cat slowly walking away, Koko is your subject."

"It was all new and strange to him," said Hixie, undaunted. "We'll try it another day."

"I'm afraid Koko will always be his own cat. He cares nothing for fame and fortune and media exposure. The word *cooperation* has never been in his vocabulary. Whenever I try to take a snapshot, he rolls over on his haunches, points one leg to heaven in a pornographic pose, and licks his intimate parts. . . . Let's go and finish our coffee."

Mrs. Cobb had a fresh pot waiting for them, and she served it in the library with a few of her apricot-almond crescents.

"What's new in the restaurant business?" Qwilleran asked Hixie.

"Not much. We've just hired a busboy named Derek Cuttlebrink. I love funny names. In school I knew a Betty Schipps, who married a man named Fisch, and they opened a seafood restaurant. Do you ever browse through the Moose County phone book? It's a panic! Fugtree, Mayfus, Inchpot, Hackpole . . ."

"I know Hackpole," said Qwilleran. "He's in used cars and auto repair."

"Then let me tell you something amusing. When I first took this job I was trying to be ever so charming, remembering faces and greeting customers by name. I'd taken a course to improve my memory, and I was using the association technique. One day Mr. Hackpole came in with some frumpy woman that he was trying to impress, and I called him Mr. Chopstick. He didn't like it one bit."

"He has no sense of humor," Qwilleran said, lowering his voice, "and that 'frumpy woman' happens to be Mrs. Cobb, the housekeeper of my choice, whose apricot-almond crescents you're wolfing down."

"I'm sorry, but you have to admit she's frumpy," Hixie whispered.

"Not any frumpier than a certain advertising woman I used to know Down Below."

"Touché," she said. "Why don't you come to the Mill for lunch today?"

"What's the special?"

"Chili. Bring your own fire extinguisher."

Shortly before noon Qwilleran had another visitor. Nick Bamba, husband of his part-time secretary in Mooseville, dropped off a batch of letters to be signed. Nick was greeted effusively by two sniffing Siamese, who seemed to know that he shared living quarters with three cats and a person whose long braids were tied with dangling ribbons. The two men went into the library followed by two vertical brown tails, stiff with importance.

"Time for a drink?" Qwilleran asked. He welcomed the visits of the sharp-eyed young engineer who worked at the state prison and shared his interest in crime. "How's everything at the incarceration facility?"

"Quiet enough to have me worried," Nick said. "Make it bourbon. How do you like this weather?"

"It reached six below in Brrr the other night."

"Windchill factor was thirty-five below."

"How's the baby?" Qwilleran could never remember the name or sex of the Bamba offspring.

"He's fine. He's a good baby, and healthy, thank God!"

"That's good to know. Did you take Snuffles to the vet?"

"He says it's some kind of dermatitis that affects spayed cats. She's taking hormones now."

"I appreciated your report on the trespasser, Nick. I notified the sheriff as you suggested."

"I see you've got your property posted now."

"Mr. O'Dell hurried up there and covered all the bases: no trespassing, no hunting, no camping."

"He's a terrific guy," Nick said. "When I was in high school he bailed me out of some hairy scrapes."

"Anything new in Mooseville?"

"There's never anything new in Mooseville. But . . . you know that camper I spotted on your property last week? It was unusual for this area—sort of citified. Three shades of brown. Custom job. Since then I've seen it several times in the parking lot at the Old Stone Mill, back near the kitchen door. Just for the hell of it, I did a rundown on the plates. It's registered to someone by the name of Hixie Rice."

After Nick had left, Qwilleran reflected that Hixie was hardly the outdoor type; he had never seen her in heels lower than three inches.

He went to lunch early and ordered his bowl of chili.

"Did Koko get over his snit?" Hixie asked.

"Apparently. As soon as you walked out the door, he gobbled the pork liver cupcake. . . . Incidentally, who owns that good-looking camper on the parking lot?"

Hixie looked vague. "The brown one? Oh, it belongs to one of our cooks. Her husband works in Mooseville and has to commute sixty miles a day, so he drives their small car, and she drives the gas-guzzler to work."

What was she hiding? Qwilleran recalled that Hixie had always been a glib liar, though not necessarily a successful one, and she always managed to get involved with a certain fringe element in the romance department. What else had she invented? The invisible chef? His cookbook? His sick mother in Philadelphia?

ELEVEN

Wednesday, November twentieth. When the telephone rang at six in the morning, Qwilleran knew it would be Harry Noyton. Who else would have the nerve or insensitivity to call at that hour? He managed a sleepy hello and heard an unbearably cheerful voice say, "Rise and shine! Gonna sleep all day? How about inviting me over for one of those he-man breakfasts?"

"Do you expect me to get the housekeeper out of bed in the middle of the night?" Qwilleran grumbled.

"I'm coming over there anyway. Want to talk to you. I'll grab a taxi and be there in five minutes."

"There are no taxis, Harry. You can walk. It's only three blocks."

"I haven't walked three blocks since they let me out of the infantry!"

"Try it! It's good for you. Don't go to the main house; come to my apartment over the garage."

Qwilleran pulled on some clothes and opened a closet door that concealed a mini kitchen. A mini sink produced instant boiling water for his culinary specialty, instant coffee. A mini microwave thawed breakfast rolls taken from a mini freezer.

In no time at all Noyton bounded up the stairs. "Is this where you live? I like this modern stuff better than the junk in the big house. Hey, this is a sexy sofa! Do you bring girls up here?"

Qwilleran was always grumpy before his morning coffee. "This is where I work, Harry. I'm writing a book."

"No jive! What's it about?"

"You'll have to wait and buy a copy when it's published."

"I like you newspaper guys," said Noyton with buoyant good humor. "You're independent! That's why I go for this idea of owning a paper. This neck of the woods is waiting for something to happen. There's a lot of money up here! People own their own planes, three or four cars, forty-foot boats, sable coats! You should see the rocks on the women at the country club!"

"You're looking at inherited wealth," Qwilleran

said. "There's also poverty and unemployment, and too many kids aren't going to college. A newspaper with guts could stir up some civic consciousness and promote job training and job opportunities and scholarships. The Klingenschoen Fund can't do it alone—and shouldn't do it alone!"

"Dammit! You've got it all figured out. That's what I like about you newspaper guys."

Qwilleran placed mugs of coffee and a plate of Mrs. Cobb's cinnamon rolls on the travertine card table. "Pull up a chair, Harry. How do you like the hotel? Are you comfortable?"

"Hell, they gave me the bridal suite with a round bed and pink satin sheets!"

"What luck with your conferences yesterday?"

"No hitch! Everything's sewed up! That Goodwinter gal doesn't know what hit her! I wrote six-figure checks on three different banks for the rights to the *Picayune* name and the old printing equipment."

"How did you work it?"

"The mayor took us all to lunch at the club—her and the economic development guys—private conference room. It was upbeat all the way. When it was over, she was calling me Harry and I was calling her Gritty. My lawyers called her lawyer, her banker called my bankers, and we both had a deal. The city's behind it a hundred percent. It'll create jobs. We get a building tax-free for ten years. The paper can be job-printed until the plant is set up."

"What will happen to the old burned-out building?"

"The city's condemning it and paying her off. They'll resell it for a minimall. The county commissioners got in the act, too. The county will go fifty-fifty on a newspaper museum near Mooseville. Tourist attraction, you know. . . . Hey, these are damn good rolls!"

"What was XYZ Enterprises doing all the time you were outbidding them and buttering up the widow?"

"XYZ never had anything on paper. It was all hanky-panky with Gritty. So she wasn't obligated to do business with those robbers. If a poor widow can get three-quarters of a million instead of some piddling five-digit figure, who's going to take her to court?"

Qwilleran thought, The news won't go down well with Exbridge. She'll have to move out of Indian Village in a hurry. The news will be all over town by now.

Noyton was wound up and talking nonstop. "Some of the commissioners drove me around to see the lay of the land, and—hey, you faker!—they didn't say a word about rutting bucks coming through the windshield! I like Mooseville. Everything's built of logs. I'd like to build a hotel there. The town's ripe for a highrise. We could build it of poured concrete logs. How does that grab you?"

"Harry, you have no taste. Leave the design to the architects."

"Hell, it's my money! I tell the architects what to design."

"Well, when the newspaper is launched, don't try to tell the editors how to edit."

Noyton's face took on a confidential smirk. "Gritty rode with us to Mooseville, and we sat in the back seat and developed a little—what do you call it?"

"Rapport."

"Then she took me to dinner at the place with the wheel that rattles and creaks. I told them to give me an oilcan and a screwdriver, and I'd go out and fix the damn thing. But we had a good time, Qwill, and I mean a *go-o-od* time. We ended up in my suite at the hotel with a bottle of hooch. She didn't want to go home to where she's been living, so I made a little arrangement at the hotel. Couldn't let those pink sheets go to waste. She's my kind of woman, Qwill—with spunk and a little shape to her figure. Remember Natalie? My life was never the same after I lost Natalie. And do you know what? Gritty goes for me in a big way! I'm taking her to Hawaii for a little holiday. I've got some business down there. Nothing big. Just condos."

"You'd better get out of here before snow flies," Qwilleran said, "and before Exbridge comes after you with a shotgun. He just got a divorce because of Gritty."

"I'm not afraid of Exbridge," Noyton said. "I've handled smarter suckers than him. . . . Oh, by the way, I talked to your editor friend—found him down in Texas—and he's hot for it. Then Gritty took me to the hospital to meet Junior, and he went into orbit!"

Qwilleran said, "Find out if Gritty knows anything about a small fireproof box that disappeared in the *Picayune* fire. No one knows what it contains, but Junior thinks it's important. It could be buried in the rubble."

"No problem! We'll get a crew over there and start sifting. And did I tell you I made an offer for the Pickax Hotel? We'll get a good decorator up here from Down Below and change the name to Noyton House."

"Don't do it that way. Use a local designer and keep the old name. Do you want these good people to think they're being invaded? The trick is to fit in, not take over."

"Okay, General. Yes *sir*, General. Sure you don't want to go on my payroll?"

"No, thanks."

"Now I've got to get out of here. Thanks for the coffee. I've tasted better, but it was sure strong! I've got a few loose ends to tie up before I leave for the airport. I've chartered a plane to Minneapolis."

"Need a ride to the airport?"

Noyton shook his head and looked smug. "Gritty's driving me, but do me a favor, will you? She'll leave her car keys at the terminal desk with Charlie. Somebody should pick it up before snow flies. She won't be needing it. She's not coming back till spring."

Noyton had just gone thumping down the stairs in his new boots when Junior telephoned. "Want to hear some news?"

"Good or bad?"

"Both. The deal for the *Picayune* is finalized. The money's in the bank. Arch Riker is on his way up here. I'm getting out of the hospital today. I've shaved off my beard, and Grandma Gage is going to Florida, so I'm house-sitting till she comes back."

"What's the bad news?"

"Jody's mad at me. I don't know what's wrong with her. All of a sudden she says I don't listen to her and I ignore her when other people are around."

"You'll have to start thinking from her viewpoint as well as your own if you two are going to get married," Qwilleran said. "I speak from sad experience. You don't know how much she worries about you. She worried about you when your father died, when you were fighting the *Picayune* fire, when you missed out at the *Fluxion*, and when you went out in the woods."

There was a pause, then, "Maybe you're right, Qwill."

At eight o'clock Qwilleran tuned in the morning weather report: "Storm warnings in effect for all of Moose County. . . . Repeat: Storm warnings in effect."

Mrs. Cobb buzzed him on the intercom. "Are you interested in breakfast, Mr. Q?"

"Not this morning, thanks, but I want to talk with you before you leave for the auction."

He put the Siamese in the wicker hamper, and the three of them crossed the yard to the main house.

"Did you hear the weather report?" Mrs. Cobb said. "It sounds like the Big One. I hope it holds off until after the auction. Susan Exbridge is picking me up at ten o'clock. Herb told me not to buy anything, but you know how I am at auctions!"

"How was the preview?"

"They have some wonderful things, and I saw the farmhouse for the first time. I can hardly wait to get my hands on it. We solved our problem; Herb is going to have one wing of the house for smoking and guns and stuffed moose heads and all that. Are you going to the auction?"

"I might drop in for a while to see the action. When's the best time to go?"

"Not too early. They put up box lots in the morning and hold the good things till later. They'll have a lunch wagon around noon. Don't forget to dress warm, and don't wear your best clothes, Mr. Q."

After Mrs. Cobb had bustled off in great excitement Qwilleran loitered around the house until he could stand the suspense no longer. Who would be at the auction? What were they buying? How high were the prices? What were people talking about? What were they serving at the lunch wagon? Wearing his lumberjack coat, woodsman's hat, and duck boots, he headed for Black Creek Lane in North Middle Hummock.

The country roads were unusually heavy with traffic. Cars, vans, and pickups were heading north, and a few were returning, loaded. Half a mile from the farmhouse he began to see vehicles parked on both sides of the road. He pulled in where a pickup was pulling out and walked the rest of the way. Auction-goers were trudging to their cars lugging floor lamps and rocking chairs. One woman was carrying a fern stand made of bent twigs.

"I don't care, honey," she said to her frowning spouse. "I simply wanted something that belonged to a Goodwinter, even if it was only an old toothbrush."

Parked in the front yard was a moving van labeled Foxy Fred's Bid-a-Bit Auctions. Customers shuffled through rustling leaves, examining rows of household furnishings: blankets, bicycles, small appliances, glassware, laundry equipment, garden tools. Large pieces of furniture were still in the farmhouse; everything else was jammed into a large pole barn where the bidding was in full swing.

Foxy Fred, wearing a western hat and red down jacket, was on the platform, haranguing a hundred or more bidders who were packed in shoulder-to-shoulder. "Here's a genuwine old barn lantern complete with wick. Who'll gimme five? . . . Five? . . . Gimme four . . . Dollar bill over there. Gimme two. Gimme two. . . . Two I got. Gimme three. Do I see three? Three! No money! Wanna four, wanna four, wanna four."

In order to bid, customers were picking up numbered flashcards from a red-jacketed woman who was entering sales in a ledger and collecting money. Qwilleran had no intention of bidding, but he picked up a card anyway. It was number 124.

"Look up! Look up!" the auctioneer called out. Porters in red Bid-a-Bit windbreakers were hoisting an upholstered chair high over their heads for audience inspection.

Bidding was slow, however. The customers were either bored or stifled by blasts of heat from portable electric heaters. Suddenly Foxy Fred jolted them to attention. After only two bids he allowed a ladder-back rocker to go for an outrageously low price. The audience protested.

"If you don't like it, wake up and bid!" he scolded them.

Qwilleran ambled out of the barn and found Mrs. Cobb and Susan Exbridge at the lunch wagon. "How's the food?" he asked.

"It's not exactly Old Stone Mill," said Mrs. Exbridge, "but it's good. Try the bratwurst. It's homemade."

"The new chef at the Mill has made a big difference," Qwilleran said. "Has anyone met him?"

"I've seen him in the parking lot at Indian Village," she said. "He's tall, blond, and *very* good-looking, but he seems rather shy."

Mrs. Cobb said, "You'll never guess what I bought! A handmade cherry cradle! I'm expecting my first grandchild soon."

"Are the out-of-state dealers bidding things up?" Qwilleran asked her.

"They're hanging back, waiting for the good items, but there's a lot of them here. I can always spot a dealer. They're sort of shrewd-looking but laid-back. See that short man with his hands in his pockets? See the woman with a fuzzy brown hat? They're dealers. The man in the shearing coat—I think he's security. He isn't bidding. He isn't even listening. He's just watching people."

Before turning to look, Qwilleran had a hunch it would be the stranger who claimed to be a historian. The man was wandering aimlessly through the crowd.

At that moment there was a general movement toward the barn, as if on signal. Inside the building the chatter was loud and excited as the porters started to bring out the heavy artillery.

"Look up! Look up!" the auctioneer shouted in a voice that cut through the hubbub. "Victorian rococo chair, genuwine Belter, I think—part of a parlor suite—two chairs and a settee. Upholstered in black horsehair. Good condition. Who'll gimme two thousand for the set? Two thousand to start. Two thousand, anyone?"

A flash card was raised.

"HEP!" shouted a porter, who doubled as spotter.

"Two thousand I got. Gimme twenty-five gimme twenty-five gimme twenty-five. Waddala waddala waddala . . ."

"HEP!"

"Twenty-five! Gimme thirty."

"HEP!"

"Thirty! Gimme forty. Waddala waddala bidda waddala bidda bidda waddala . . ."

"HEP!"

The excitement was mounting. It was like the last half of the ninth inning with the score tied, two out, and the bases loaded, Qwilleran thought. It was like third down on the two-yard line with a minute to play.

When the furniture was finally knocked down for a figure that he considered astronomical, the audience deflated with groans and sighs.

Someone tugged at his sleeve, and a woman's voice said, "How come you didn't bid on that one, Qwill?"

"Hixie! I didn't know you liked auctions!"

"I don't, but my customers have been talking about this one, so I sneaked away when the lunch crowd thinned out."

"Quiet back there!" shouted Foxy Fred, and Qwilleran took Hixie's arm and steered her outside and across the yard to the farmhouse.

"The good stuff is in here," he said, picking up a catalogue. Among the large items still in the house were two General Grant beds, a parlor organ, a breakfront twelve feet wide, a large pine hutch, a black walnut sideboard with matching table, and a ponderous rolltop desk. "This desk is the only thing I'd be tempted to bid on," Qwilleran told Hixie.

She was not really interested in the antiques. "Have you heard the latest rumor?" she asked.

"Which one? The town is full of rumors this week."

"It's no false alarm. My boss's live-in friend is eloping with another man. They came in for dinner last night—a couple of middle-aged lovebirds acting like kids. I seated them at a good table over the waterwheel, and it drove the guy crazy. He asked for an oilcan."

"Does Exbridge know about the switch?"

"Apparently, because he's livid! When he came in for lunch today he was in a mood for murder. The Bloody Mary was warm; the soup was cold; the veal was tough. He threatened to fire Antoine."

"Who?"

"Well, he likes to be called Tony, but his name is Antoine."

Qwilleran was fingering the flash card in his pocket. "I've got to go back to the barn to see what's happening," he said. "See you later."

The mood in the barn was contagious. He was catching auction fever, the symptoms being nervous excitement and a reckless sense of adventure.

"It's getting hot now, folks," shouted Foxy Fred, and an oak icebox, an eighteenth-century candlestand, and a Queen Anne table went under the hammer in rapid succession. Then the parlor organ and pine hutch were auctioned by number from the catalogue.

"Next we have a six-foot rolltop desk in cherry-wood," said the auctioneer. "Perfect condition. Dated 1881. Outstanding provenance. Belonged to Ephraim Goodwinter, mine owner, lumberman, founder of the *Pickax Picayune*, and donor of the Pickax Public Library. Shall we start at five thousand? . . . Five thousand? . . . *Four* thousand?"

"One thousand," said a woman near the platform. It was the dealer with the fuzzy brown hat.

"One thousand I've got. No money! Beautiful desk—seven drawers—lots of pigeonholes—maybe a secret compartment. Who'll bid two thousand?"

Qwilleran held up his card.

"HEP!" shouted the spotter.

"Two thousand now. Make it three. Three do I hear? Solid cherry. Lotta history goes with this desk."

"HEP!"

"Three thousand we got. Who'll bid three and a half? Waddala waddala bidda waddala bidda bidda bidda waddala . . ."

The auctioneer's singsong gibberish had a mesmerizing effect on Qwilleran. He raised his card.

"Thirty-five hundred for this five-thousand-dollar desk, folks. No money. Make it four-triple-oh, four-triple-oh, four-triple-oh . . ."

"HEP!"

Qwilleran's turtleneck jersey was tightening around his neck. He slipped out of his coat.

"Four thousand. Make it fournahaff fournahaff fournahaff. It's a giveaway. Solid cherry. Cast brasses."

"HEP!"

"Four thousand five hundred. Do I hear five grand? It's going, folks. Are you gonna let 'em steal it?"

"Forty-six!" Quilleran called out.

"Four-six! Who'll gimme four-seven? Waddala waddala bidda waddala bidda bidda waddala . . ."

"HEP!"

The woman in the fuzzy brown hat wanted the desk and was inching up.

"Four-seven. Do I hear four-eight? Waddala waddala bidda . . ."

Qwilleran raised his card.

"HEP!"

"Four thousand eight hundred. It's going, folks—"

"Forty-nine!" said the dealer.

"Fifty!" shouted Qwilleran.

"That's the spirit! Do I hear fifty-one?"

All heads turned to the dealer in the fuzzy hat. The hat wagged a negative.

"Fifty-one do I hear? Fifty-one? Going for five thousand. Going going going . . . SOLD to number one twenty-four."

The audience applauded. Mrs. Cobb waved her catalogue in wild approval. Qwilleran mopped his brow.

After making arrangements to have the desk delivered, he drove home in a confused state of shock and agitation. Five thousand for a piece of furniture still seemed like a staggering sum to the former feature writer for the *Daily Fluxion*. At a restaurant in Middle Hummock he tried to phone Junior, but there was no answer at Grandma Gage's house.

Upon arriving home, he discovered why. There was a message on the answering machine. "Hi! We're flying Down Below to get married. Jody's parents live near Cleveland. Hope we get back before snow flies. And hey! They found Dad's lockbox!"

Mrs. Cobb had gone out to dinner with Susan Exbridge, so Qwilleran rummaged in the refrigerator and found some lentil soup and cold chicken. He heated the soup for himself and cut up the chicken for the Siamese.

"No readings tonight," he told Koko. "I've had enough stimulation for one day. *'The rest is silence.'* That's from *Hamlet*, in case you didn't know."

The tall case clock in the foyer bonged seven times, and he tuned in the weather report. Storm warnings had been in effect all day, and yet the weather had been fine. Dubiously he listened to the current prediction:

"Storm warnings were lifted late this afternoon, but a storm alert remains in effect. Winds are twenty-five miles an hour, gusting to forty. Present temperature: nineteen in Pickax, seven in Brrr. And now for a look at the headlines. . . . Two persons were killed in a car-deer accident on Airport Road at four forty-five p.m. Names are withheld pending notification of relatives. The westbound car struck and killed a large buck, then entered a ditch ..."

"*Junior!*" Qwilleran cried. "No! No! The *Picayune* jinx! Fifth to die a violent death! And poor little Jody ..."

TWELVE

Thursday, November twenty-first. "Storm warnings are again in effect for Moose County," said the WPKX announcer, "with high winds continuing from the northwest and temperatures constant in the twenties. . . . And in the news . . . here's an update on yesterday's fatal accident in the Airport Road. Killed at four forty-five p.m. were Gertrude Goodwinter, forty-eight, of North Middle Hummock, and Harold Noyton, fifty-two, of Chicago. According to the sheriff's department, their car struck and killed a large buck, then entered a ditch and rolled over."

Qwilleran made an early visit to the police station that morning to see Andrew Brodie. Although the sheriff's deputies were courteous and cooperative, only the Pickax police chief could be depended upon for friendly conversation and off-the-record information.

Brodie was sitting at his desk, swamped with paperwork and complaining as usual. "And what's on your mind?" he asked, after a tirade about computer systems.

"Do you know anything about yesterday's fatal accident on Airport Road?"

"The sheriff and state police handled it," he said, "but we helped track down the next of kin. Wasn't easy, what with her husband just buried and her mother in Florida and Junior on a plane somewhere and the other two kids out west. The fellah that was with her—they had to get lawyers and bankers out of bed to find out about him."

"At first I thought Junior and Jody had been killed. I knew Jody is a friend of your daughter's, so I tried calling your house last night but got no answer."

"The wife and I were out visiting," Brodie said, "and Francesca was rehearsing for that concert at the church, where they're going to wear all those old-fashioned costumes. It'll be a spectacle, all right. They're making their own costumes, and they're going all out!"

"I'm looking forward to it," Qwilleran said, after which he commented on the weather, the hunting season, and the Goodwinter auction before steering the conversation back to the accident. "Do you know who was driving?"

"No telling. They were both thrown from the car, as I understand it."

"I assume they weren't wearing seat belts."

"It would look like it, wouldn't it?"

"Does the sheriff think they were traveling fast?"

"According to the skid marks, pretty fast. And according to the coroner, they'd had a few. The buck was a big one, over two hundred pounds, eight-point. Don't suppose you know anything about the fellah she was with. The name's Noyton."

"All I know," Qwilleran said, "is that he's a one-man conglomerate with some greedy ex-wives and squabbling children, and they'll be challenging the will for ten years."

When he left Brodie's office, Qwilleran began wondering how Exbridge would react to Gritty's death, and how the ex—Mrs. Exbridge would react to her ex-husband's loss of his ex-mistress. His curiosity prompted him to have lunch again at the Old Stone Mill. Hixie was always good for some candid observations.

Today she seemed nervous and preoccupied, however. She seated guests but avoided conversation. Qwilleran took a long time to consume his pea soup and corned beef sandwich, stalling until most of the customers had left. Then he offered to buy Hixie a drink, and she sat down at his table in a fretful mood.

"Hideous accident on Airport Road," he remarked. "Wasn't the woman your boss's former roommate?"

"I can't worry about his problems today," she snapped. "I have problems of my own."

"What's the matter?"

"Tony left suddenly this morning—right before the lunch rush! No explanation. He just went out the window."

"The window?"

"And he took *my car*! *My car* instead of that stupid camper!"

"I thought the camper belonged to one of your cooks."

Hixie dismissed the question with a wave of the hand. "It was in my name. That is, I bought it for *his birthday*. So why didn't he take the camper? Why did he take *my* car?"

"Perhaps he had some urgent errand to do."

"Then why did he go out the washroom window? And why did he take his *knives*? I see what it's all about, Qwill—the same old shaft for big-hearted Hixie. If Tony planned to come back, he wouldn't have taken his *knives*. You know how chefs are about their knives. They practically *sleep* with them."

"Did anything unusual happen to cause his quick exit?"

Hixie frowned at her glass of Campari before answering. "Well, about eleven o'clock we were setting up for lunch, and a man hammered on the door. It was locked, and one of the waitresses went to see what he wanted. He asked for Antoine Delapierre. She told him we had no one by that name, but he barged right in. I was folding napkins at the serving station, and I could tell right away he wasn't just another *potato chip* salesman. He looked cold and determined."

"Was he wearing a shearling car coat and rabbit-fur hat?"

"Something like that. Anyway, I asked what he wanted, and he said he was a friend of Antoine Delapierre. Tony heard it, grabbed his knives, and bolted into the employees' washroom. That's the last we saw of him. He left the window open and blazed away in *my* car! Why did I ever give that jerk a duplicate set of keys?"

Because he was tall, blond, and very good-looking, Qwilleran thought. He felt sorry for her. Hixie, the born loser, had lost out again. But this time she wasn't weeping; she was furious.

"Then Tony Peters wasn't his real name?" he asked.

"A lot of people change their names for business purposes," she said casually, but her eyes were shifting nervously.

"Do you know what the incident was all about?"

"I haven't the *foggiest* idea. When the man walked into the kitchen, I got huffy and ordered him out."

Qwilleran refrained from pursuing the conversation. Sooner or later Hixie would blurt out the truth. He contemplated the new development with some satisfaction. His suspicion had checked out; the stranger in Pickax was actually an investigator.

Meanwhile, he had to go home and dress for dinner at Polly Duncan's cottage on MacGregor Road. Roast beef and Yorkshire pudding!

Mrs. Cobb was busy in the kitchen, baking hazelnut jumbles. "Do you think you should drive out in the country, Mr. Q?" she said. "They mentioned storm warnings on the radio."

"They mentioned storm warnings on the radio yesterday, and nothing happened. I think their computer is malfunctioning. They've been reading last year's weather predictions all month. So there's nothing to worry about."

He took a handful of hazelnut jumbles and went looking for the Siamese. He made it a point to say goodbye to them whenever he left the house for a few hours—another of Lori Bamba's recommendations.

The cats were not in the library, but a copy of *The Tempest* lay on the floor beneath the bust of Shakespeare. It gave Qwilleran pause, but only for a moment. Koko had pulled out that threatening title once before, and there had been no stormy weather. Senior Goodwinter had crashed into the old plank bridge, but the weather remained fine.

Qwilleran headed north. It was cold, and there was a high wind, but he was wearing his suede car coat with beaver collar, a trooper's hat in the same fur, a wool shirt in the Mackintosh tartan, hunting boots, fur-lined choppers, and, of course, the long red underwear that was standard equipment in Moose County.

The sky was overcast, and the wind whistled, but his heart was light and his mind was fired with ambition. After this evening he would plunge into the writing of the book he had neglected; it would please Polly to know he was writing again.

Her invitation to dinner was auspicious; it meant, he hoped, that she was relaxing the mystifying behavior that kept him at arm's length. He thought he had discovered the reason for her reserve. At a recent meeting of the library board a grant from the Klingenschoen Fund was allocated to the purchase of books, video equipment, and a new furnace—not a dollar for personnel. Furthermore, he was appalled to learn how little the head librarian was paid. Polly's tiny cottage, old car, and limited wardrobe all suggested straitened circumstances. Qwilleran knew her to be a proud woman; did the discrepancy in their financial status embarrass her? He knew—and she undoubtedly knew—that the town gossips would enjoy labeling the head librarian a gold digger.

With these thoughts running through his mind as he drove, he hardly noticed the minuscule dots of white on his windshield. A little farther on, large snowflakes in crystalline designs reminded him of a childhood thrill—catching them on his tongue. Soon a light dusting of snow was visible on the pavement, and Qwilleran slowed his speed to allow for slippery patches.

By the time he turned off the main highway onto MacGregor Road, there was a veil of white over fields and evergreens—a beautiful sight, although swirling snow was obscuring his vision. Dusk seemed to be falling early. He was now traveling east, and the snow was whipping against the windshield fast enough to render the wipers ineffective. It was just a snow squall, he told himself. It wouldn't last long. He drove slowly and carefully.

Polly's house, he remembered from his previous, surreptitious visit, was three miles from the main highway—two miles of pavement, then a jog in the road, and a mile of gravel. There were no other cars in sight, and he was now driving through a tunnel of white—dense white. He hoped he could stay on the pavement; there were no tire tracks to follow. No one had passed that way since the snow had started to fall. Crossroads were indistinguishable from open fields.

Suddenly something loomed up in front of his car, and he stopped just before plunging into underbrush. He had reached the jog in the road. Now he had to turn left for a short distance and then turn right onto the unimproved continuation of MacGregor Road. He made several attempts before finding the actual turn. After that he knew it would be clear sailing—just a mile to the two rural mailboxes, MacGregor and Duncan. He checked the odometer.

The problem was to stay on the road; on each

side of the roadbed would be the inevitable drainage ditch. The windshield wipers, though working furiously, were useless against the onslaught of snow. He was driving through a white blanket. The hood of the car was invisible. At least he didn't have to worry about deer; they would be driven to cover. He had learned that much from Hackpole. But he had no time to think about Hackpole, or even Polly. The problem was to drive in a straight line while blinded by snow.

Again a clump of vegetation loomed up ahead. He was off the road! Turning the wheel, he went into a skid. He babied it, but the car was sliding sideways. It was sliding down a slope, and it came to a stop at a dangerous angle. The drainage ditch! Another degree of tilt, and the car would roll over. He turned off the ignition and sat there, surrounded on all sides by walls of white.

He knew the car would never make it out of the ditch under those slippery conditions—and from that angle—even with front-wheel drive. He considered the options. The longer he hesitated, the more the snow banked up against the windshield and side window—an opaque layer, inches thick, and gray-white in the dusk. Opening the door, he tested the terrain underfoot. Slush! It was the ditch. If he scrambled up the slope he would be on solid ground, and he could walk the rest of the way. It was now less than half a mile, he knew.

Putting on his hat, pulling down the earflaps, turning up his coat collar, tugging on the mittens, he prepared to face the elements. If he clambered up the bank and turned right, he would be headed toward the farm. He would have to proceed on blind faith. In the enveloping blizzard there was no sense of direction; the wind was hurling snow from all points of the compass.

Now he could feel something solid underfoot—the roadbed—but already there was an accumulation of five, ten, or fifteen inches, depending on the drifting. He moved forward, blinded by the snow, one thoughtful step at a time. He had a plan! If he found himself slipping down a slope to the right, he would be off the roadbed; he would veer to the left. If he slipped to the left, he would be headed for the opposite ditch.

In this way he zigzagged ahead, not daring to hope that a car would come along. Would he see the fog lights? Would he hear the motor above the howling wind? It was shrieking now, shrieking through trees that he couldn't see.

Though his coat collar and storm hat were snug, and though his trousers were stuffed into his boots, the relentless wetness found its way into every crevice. He banged the snow off his mittens and brushed the buildup from his face. It was no use; in another few seconds he was coated with freezing wet.

He had been walking for what seemed like an hour. Could he be traveling in a circle? If he had inadvertently done a right-about-face, thinking the right ditch was the left ditch, he would now be headed for the main highway, three miles back.

The blind groping was discouraging, frightening. He was totally disoriented. He held his mittened hands in front of him like a sleepwalker, but there was nothing to feel. He could hardly keep his eyes open. His eyelids were raw. Were they freezing shut? His cheeks and forehead were numb from the vicious wind and wet. He shouted, "Hello!" He shouted, "Help!" He was shouting into a void and swallowing snow.

What do I do now? he asked himself—not in panic but in defeat. He had an overbearing desire to sink to his knees, roll up in a ball, and call it quits. Keep going, he told himself. Keep going!

He remembered the mailboxes. He had to bump into them, or he'd miss them entirely. He inched along, not seeing, not feeling, not knowing. The snow was getting deeper underfoot and piling inches thick on his clothing. He stood still and tried to breathe normally, but he was being smothered by the wind and drowned by the snow.

Suddenly, without warning, something rose up in front of him and he fell over two mailboxes, close together, with a foot of snow on top of each. He threw his arms around them like a drowning sailor clutching at floating debris. He bent over them, trying to catch his breath.

A few feet beyond would be the driveway. But how many feet beyond? It was trial and error. When he banged a knee on a concrete culvert, he knew he was there. He remembered a hedge that bordered the drive. He would follow the hedge, feeling his way. It worked until the hedge came to an abrupt end. The brick farmhouse would be on the left. The cottage should be straight ahead.

Once again he was stumbling blindly on what he hoped would be a straight course. It was dark now, and he realized that snow is not white in the black of night. Yet, he thought he detected a glow in the space ahead. He followed it, reaching for it, until he fell over steps buried in a drift. He scrambled up on hands and knees. There was a door directly in front of him. He leaned against it, pounding with both fists. The door opened, and he fell into a kitchen.

"Oh, my God! Qwill! What happened? Are you hurt?"

He was on his hands and knees in an avalanche of snow jolted from his clothing when he fell. Polly was tugging at his arm. He crawled farther into the room and heard the door slam behind him, cutting off the noise of the storm. It was bright and quiet indoors.

"Are you all right? Can you get up? I didn't think you were coming. What happened to your car?"

He wanted to stay on the floor, but he allowed her to help him to his feet.

"Let me brush you off. Stand still."

He stood, silent and motionless, while she pulled off his hat and mittens and threw them on the kitchen table. With towels she removed the snow and ice from his moustache and eyebrows. She brushed a bushel of snow from his coat, pants, and boots. And still he stood, dumbly and numbly, in a flood of melting snow and ice.

Now she was untoggling his car coat. "Let's get you out of these wet clothes, and I'll get you a hot drink. Sit down. Let me pull your boots off."

She led him to a chair, and he sat obediently.

"Your socks are dry. Do your feet feel all right? They're not numb, are they? Your shirt is wet around the collar. I'll put it in the dryer. Your pants, too. They're soaking wet. Thank the Lord you wore long johns. I'll bring you some blankets."

And still he could say nothing. She wrapped him in blankets and led him to a sofa, convinced him to lie down, tucked him in, stuck a thermometer in his mouth.

"I'm going to make some hot tea and call the doctor to see if I'm doing the right thing."

Qwilleran closed his eyes and thought of nothing but warmth and dryness and safety. Vaguely he heard a teakettle whistling, a telephone being jiggled, water being sponged into a pail.

When Polly returned with a mug of hot tea on a tray, she said, "The phone's dead. The lines must be down. I wonder if I should bring you a warm footbath. How do you feel? Do you want to sit up and drink some tea?" She took the thermometer from his mouth and studied it.

Qwilleran was beginning to feel like himself. He rose to a sitting position without assistance. He accepted the mug of tea with a grateful glance at Polly. He sipped it and uttered a long, deep sigh. Then he spoke his first words. *"For this relief, much thanks, for it is bitter cold."*

"Thank God!" She laughed and cried. "You're alive! What a fright you gave me! But you're all right. When you quote Shakespeare, I know you're all right."

She threw her arms around his blanketed shoulders and nestled her head on his chest. At that moment the power failed. Half of Moose County blacked out, and the cottage was thrown into darkness.

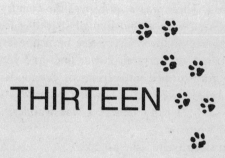

THIRTEEN

Friday, November twenty-second. Qwilleran opened his eyes in a small bedroom filled with dazzling light.

"Wake up, Qwill! Wake up! Come and see what's happened!" Someone in a blue robe was standing at the window, gazing rapturously at the scene outdoors. "We've had an ice storm!"

He was slow to wake, Groggily he remembered the night before: Polly . . . her tiny cottage . . . the blizzard.

"Don't lie there, Qwill. Come and see. It's beautiful!"

"You're beautiful," he said. "Life is beautiful!"

It was cool in the bedroom, although a comforting rumble and roar somewhere in the cottage indicated that the space heater was operating. Dragging himself out of bed, he wrapped himself in a blanket, and joined Polly at the window.

What he saw was an enchanted landscape, dazzlingly bright in a cold, hard November sun. The wind was still. There was a hush over the countryside, now glazed with a thin film of sparkling ice. Fields were acres of silver. Every tree branch, every twig was coated with crystal. Power lines and wire fences were transformed into strings of diamonds.

"I can't believe we had a howling blizzard last night," he said. "I can't believe I was wandering around in a whiteout."

"Did you sleep well?" she asked.

"*Very* well. And not because of tramping through the snow or eating too much roast beef. . . . I smell something good."

"Coffee," she said, "and scones in the oven."

The scones were dotted with currants and served with cream cheese and gooseberry jam.

"The hedge you followed in the blizzard," Polly said, "is a row of berry bushes, planted by the MacGregors years ago. He lets the people on the next farm pick them, and then they supply us with preserves. . . . Is something bothering you, Qwill?"

"Mrs. Cobb will be worried. Is the phone working?"

"Not yet. The power came on half an hour ago."

"Do the snowplows come down this road?"

"Eventually, but we're not on their priority list. They do the city streets and main highways first."

"Have you heard anything on the radio?"

"Everything's closed—schools, stores, offices. The library won't open until Monday. All meetings are canceled. They cleared the helicopter on the hospital roof and airlifted a patient this morning. Many cars were abandoned in snowdrifts. The body of a man was found in a car that had run off the road. He was asphyxiated. Do you carry a shovel in your trunk, Qwill?"

He shook his head guiltily.

"If you're stranded, you have to clear the snow away from the tail pipe, you know, so you can run the heater."

"If we're going to be snowbound," Qwilleran said, "I'd rather be snowbound here with you than anywhere else. It's so peaceful. How did you find this place?"

"My husband was killed on this farm while he was fighting a barn fire, and the MacGregors were very kind to me. They offered me the hired man's cottage rent-free."

"What happened to the hired man?"

"He's an extinct species. The farmers have *employees* now, who live in ranch houses in town."

"Don't you worry about your landlord in weather like this?"

"He's in Florida. His son drove him to the airport on Tuesday. I have to feed his pet goose during the winter. Did you ever hear of a goose-sitter?"

The kitchen was suddenly quiet. The space heater had done its job and clicked off. The refrigerator had finished rechilling. The pump had filled the tank and was silent. Then the silence indoors and out was broken by a distant rumble.

"The snowplow!" Polly cried. "How very unusual!"

From the west window they could see plumes of snow being blown as high as the treetops. Then the machine came into view, followed by a smaller plow and a sheriff's car. The convoy stopped in front of the farmhouse, and the small plow started on the driveway. Eventually the sheriff's car pulled up to the door.

"Mr. Qwilleran here?" the deputy asked.

Qwilleran presented himself. "My car's in the ditch somewhere along the road."

"Saw it," said the deputy. "I can take you into town . . . if you want to go," he added, glancing at the woman in a blue robe.

Qwilleran turned a disappointed face to Polly. "I'd better go. Will you be all right?"

She nodded. "I'll phone you as soon as the lines are repaired."

The deputy politely turned away as the two said goodbye.

Riding back to Pickax with the officer, Qwilleran said, "I guess this storm was the Big One."

"Yep."

"Did it do much damage?"

"The usual."

"How did you find me?"

"Just came looking. Got a call from the Pickax police chief and the mayor and the road commissioner." He picked up the microphone. "Car ninety-four to Dispatch. Got him!"

Pickax, the city of gray stone, was now smothered in white and glittering with ice. The Park Circle looked like a wedding cake. At the K mansion every window, door, and railing was crested with inches of snow, and Mr. O'Dell was riding the snowblower, clearing the driveways.

Mrs. Cobb greeted Qwilleran with a show of relief. "I was worried sick because of the way the cats were acting," she said. "They knew something was wrong. Koko howled all night."

"Where are they now?"

"Asleep on the refrigerator—exhausted! I didn't sleep a wink myself. It started to snow right after you left, and I was afraid you'd lose your way or get stuck. The phones were dead, but as soon as they fixed them I called everyone I knew, even the mayor."

"Mrs. Cobb, you're shaking. Sit down, and let's have a cup of tea, and I'll tell you about my experience."

When he had finished, she said, "The cats were right! They knew you were in trouble."

"All's well that ends well. I'll call Hackpole's garage to pull me out of the ditch. Now how about the wedding? Is everything going according to plan?"

"We-e-el," she said uncertainly, with her eyes lowered.

"Is anything wrong?"

"Well, Herb is starting to say he doesn't want me to work after we're married—at least, not here at the museum. He thinks I should stay at home and . . . and . . ."

"And what?"

She moistened her lips. "Do the bookkeeping for his business operations."

"WHAT!" Qwilleran shouted, "And waste your years of experience and knowledge? The man's crazy!"

"I told him there wouldn't be any wedding if I couldn't work at the museum," she said defiantly.

"Good for you! That took courage. I'm glad you asserted yourself." He knew how much she wanted a home of her own, and a husband. Not just a man. A husband.

"Anyway, he backed down, so I guess everything's okay. My wedding suit arrived—pink suede—and it's gorgeous! My son sent it from Saint Louis, and it doesn't need a single alteration. He'd be here for the wedding if the flying wasn't so iffy. Besides, they're expecting their baby any day now. I hope it's a boy."

Qwilleran preferred to avoid domestic details, but the housekeeper wanted to chatter about the wedding plans.

"Susan Exbridge is going to wear gray. I've ordered our corsages—pink roses—and pink rosebuds for you and Herb."

"I know you don't want a reception," Qwilleran said. "but we ought to crack a bottle of champagne and toast the bride and groom."

"That's what Susan said. She wants to bring some caviar and steak tartare."

At those words two sleeping brown heads on top of the refrigerator were promptly raised.

Qwilleran repressed a chuckle as he pictured Hackpole wearing a pink rosebud and reacting to fish eggs and raw meat. "How about background music?" he suggested. "We should put a cassette in the player."

"Oh, that would be lovely. Would you choose something, Mr. Q?"

The Bartered Bride, he thought. "And where do you want to hold the ceremony?"

"In the drawing room, in front of the fireplace. Let me show you what I have in mind."

They left the kitchen, followed by the Siamese, who liked to be included in domestic conferences.

"We could face the magistrate across a small table," Mrs. Cobb said. "A fire in the fireplace would make it cozy, and we'd put a bowl of pink roses on the table, to tie in with the roses in the rug."

At that moment there was an explosive snarl behind them. Koko was bushing his tail, arching his back, and showing his fangs. His ears and whiskers were sleeked backward, and his eyes had an evil slant.

"My heavens! What's wrong?" Mrs. Cobb cried.

"He's standing on the roses!" Qwilleran said. "He always avoids walking on the roses!"

"He gave me a fright."

"He's having a catfit, or seeing a ghost," Qwilleran said, but he felt an uneasy quiver on his upper lip, and he smoothed his moustache vigorously.

As they returned to the kitchen Mrs. Cobb said, "I'm so thankful that you brought me to Pickax, Mr. Q. It's been a wonderful experience, and I've met Herb, and I'm getting married among all the things I love. I'm very grateful."

"Don't get carried away, Mrs. Cobb. You've done a great job, and you deserve the best. Are you sure you don't want to take a week off?"

"No, we're just going to have dinner at the Pickax Hotel and spend our wedding night in their bridal suite," she said. "Then we'll have our honeymoon trip in the spring. Herb wants to take me fishing in northern Canada."

Qwilleran could not imagine her casting for trout any more than he could imagine Hackpole sleeping between pink satin sheets. "But you could take a week right now for rest and relaxation," he said.

"Well," she said almost apologetically, "there's a committee meeting Monday about the trimming of the Christmas tree, and Sunday night is the *Messiah* concert and reception in costume. I wouldn't miss that for anything!"

"What about Herb?"

"He won't mind. There's something on TV that he likes to watch every Sunday night."

Qwilleran had qualms about this marriage, and they were growing stronger. He would feel like a hypocrite, standing up for a man he heartily disliked, but he was doing it for Mrs. Cobb. She was always so generous with her time and effort and good cheer . . . so eager for approval and so embarrassed when praised . . . so knowledgeable in her field and yet so gullible in her emotions . . . so ready to please and adjust to the whims of others—especially a man with muscles and tattoos.

"You're still shaking, Mrs. Cobb," he said. "It's excitement and lack of sleep. Go upstairs and take it easy. I'll feed the cats and go out to dinner. And don't prepare any meals tomorrow; it's your wedding day."

She thanked him profusely and retired to her suite.

Qwilleran went into the library to select wedding music: Bach for the ceremony and Schubert with the champagne and caviar. Koko followed him and scrutinized each cassette, sniffing some and reaching for others with an uncertain paw.

"A feline librarian is bad enough," Qwilleran said. "Please! We don't want a feline disc jockey."

"Nyik nyik nyik," Koko retorted irritably, swiveling one ear forward and the other back.

The telephone rang, and the caller said, "The friendly telephone company has resumed service to the peasants on MacGregor Road."

The melodic voice made the back of Qwilleran's neck tingle. "I've been thinking about you, Polly. I've been thinking about everything."

"It turned out beautifully, Qwill, but I shudder to think of you in that whiteout."

"I've done a little shuddering myself. When can I see you again?"

"I'd like to drive in for the concert Sunday night."

"Why not pack an overnight bag? If you drive home after the concert, you'll only have to turn around and come back Monday morning. You can have your choice of suites upstairs: English, Empire, or Biedermeier."

"I think I'd like an English suite," Polly said. "I've always wanted to sleep in a four-poster bed with side curtains."

"YOW!" Koko said.

Replacing the receiver gently, Qwilleran said, "And you mind your own business, young man!"

FOURTEEN

Saturday, November twenty-third. "Cloudy skies and another three inches of snow," the weatherman was predicting. Nevertheless, the sun was shining, and Pickax was shimmering under the blanket of white that had descended on Thursday. Snow stayed white in Pickax.

When Qwilleran went to the main house to prepare the cats' breakfast, Mrs. Fulgrove and Mr. O'Dell were on the job. "Nice day for a wedding," he remarked.

"Sure, now, when it comes to marryin', the devil take the weather," said the houseman. "When I wedded herself, the heavens thundered an' the dogs howled an' the birds fell dead in the road, but for forty-five year we lived together with nary an angry word between us. An' when she went, God rest her soul, she went sudden with nary a pain or tear."

Mrs. Cobb was nervous. With no meals to prepare and no rum-raisin squares to bake, she puttered aimlessly about the house, waiting for her hair appointment. The cats were restless, too, sensing an upheaval of some kind. They prowled ceaselessly, and Koko talked to himself with private yows and iks and occasionally shoved a book off the shelf. Qwilleran was glad to escape. At two o'clock he was scheduled to interview Sarah Woolsmith.

The ninety-five-year-old farm woman was a long-term resident at the senior care facility adjoining the Pickax Hospital, two modern buildings that seemed out of place in a city of imitation castles and fortresses.

The matron at the reception desk was expecting Qwilleran. "Mrs. Woolsmith is waiting for you in the reading room," she said. "You'll have the place all to yourselves, but please limit your visit to fifteen minutes; she tires easily. She's looking forward to your interview. Not many people want to listen to elderly folks talk about the old days."

In the reading room he found a frail little woman with nervous hands, sitting in a wheelchair and clutching her shawl. She was accompanied by the volunteer who had wheeled her down from her bedroom.

"Sarah, dear, this is Mr. Qwilleran," the volunteer said slowly and clearly. "He's going to have a nice visit with you." In an aside she whispered, "She's ninety-five and has almost all her own teeth, but her eyesight is not good. She's a dear soul, and we all love her. I'll sit near the door and tell you when the time is up."

"Where are my teeth?" Mrs. Woolsmith demanded in shrill alarm.

"Your partial is in your mouth, dear, and you look lovely in your new shawl." She squeezed the old lady's arm affectionately.

Wasting no time on preliminaries, Qwilleran said, "Would you tell me what it was like to live on a farm when you were young, Mrs. Woolsmith? I'm going to turn on this tape recorder." He held up the machine for her to see, but she looked blankly in several directions.

The following interview was later transcribed:

Question: Were you born in Moose County?
I don't know why you want to talk to me. I never did any thing but live on a farm and raise a family. I had my name in the paper once when I had a burglar.
What kind of farming did you do?
It was in the paper—about the burglar—and I tore it out. It's in my purse. Where's my purse? Take it out and read it. You can read it to me. I like to hear it.
Sarah Woolsmith, 65, of Squunk Corners

*was sitting alone and knitting a sweater in her
living room last Thursday at 11:00 p.m., when
a man with a handkerchief over his face burst
in and said, "Give me all your money. I need it
bad." She gave him $18.73 from her purse, and
he fled on foot, leaving her unharmed but surprised.*

I used to knit in them days. We had seven
children, John and me, five of them boys. Two
killed in the war. John died in the big storm of
'37. Went to bring in the cows and froze to
death. Fifteen cows froze and all the chickens.
Winters was bad in them days. I have a 'lectric
blanket. Do you have a 'lectric blanket? When
I was a young girl we slep' under a pile of
quilts, my sisters and me. Mornings we looked
up to see the frost on the ceiling. It was pretty,
all sparkly. There was ice in the pitcher when
we washed our face. Sometimes we caught cold.
Ma rubbed skunk oil and goose grease on our
chests. We didn't like it. (Laughs.) My brother
shot wild rabbits, but I could chase 'em and
catch 'em. Pa was proud of me. Pa didn't have
a horse. He hitched Ma to the plow, and they
tilled the land. I didn't go to school. I helped
Ma in the kitchen. Once she was sick and I had
to feed sixteen men. I was only *this big*. Har-
vesttime, it was. They was all neighbors. Neighbors helped neighbors in them days.

Did you ever have time for . . .

Us womenfolks, we scrubbed clothes in a

washtub and made our own soap. I made vinegar and butter. We stuffed pillows with chicken feathers. We had lots of those! (Laughs.) Once a week we took a wagon to town and got the mail and bought a penny stick of horehound candy. I married John and we had a big farm. Cows, horses, pigs, chickens. We hired neighbor boys for huskin' and shellin'. Nickel an hour. The whitetails came and ate our corn. Once the grasshoppers came and ate everything. They ate the wash on the line. (Laughs.) The neighbor boys worked twelve hours a day, huskin' and shellin'.

What do you remember about . . .

Never locked our doors. Neighbor could walk in and borrow a cup of sugar. It was a neighbor boy took my money. I knowed who he was, but I didn't tell the constable. I knowed his voice. Worked on our farm sometimes.

Why didn't you tell the constable?

His name was Basil. I felt sorry for him. His father was in prison. Killed a man.

Was that the Whittlestaff family?

I peeked out the window when he took my money. It was moonlight. I saw him runnin' across our potato field. I knowed where he was headin' for. The freight train stopped at Watertown to take on water. You could hear the whistle two miles away. Boys used to jump the freight trains and run away. One boy fell on

the tracks and was killed. I never went on a
train.
End of interview.

The volunteer interrupted Mrs. Woolsmith's
monologue. "Time's up, dear. Say goodbye now, and
we'll go upstairs for our nap."

The old lady put forth a thin trembling hand, and
Qwilleran grasped it warmly in both of his, marveling that such fragile hands had once scrubbed
clothes, milked cows, and hoed potatoes.

The volunteer followed him into the hallway.
"Sarah remembers everything seventy-five years
ago," she said, "but she doesn't remember recent
events. By the way, I'm Irma Hasselrich."

"Are you related to the attorney for the
Klingenschoen Fund?"

"That's my father. He was prosecutor when Zack
Whittlestaff was convicted of killing Titus Goodwinter. Zack's boy, who robbed Sarah and ran
away, came back years later and repaid the eighteen
dollars and seventy-three cents, but she doesn't remember. He sends her chocolates every Christmas,
too. He turned out to be quite a successful man.
Changed his name, of course. If I had a name like
Basil Whittlestaff, I'd change it, too," she laughed.
"He sells used cars and runs a garage. He's ornery,
but he does good work."

Qwilleran went home to dress for the wedding.
He was not anticipating the occasion with any pleasure. He had been best man for Arch Riker twenty-

five years before, when he was young and crazy and not always sober. On that occasion he had fumbled the ring, causing the groom to drop it and causing two hundred guests to titter.

And now he was going to be best man for Basil Whittlestaff. When Hixie called him Mr. Chopstick, she was not far off base.

At five o'clock the November dusk had painted the snowy whiteness of Pickax a misty blue. At the K mansion the draperies were drawn, crystal chandeliers were alight, and Mr. O'Dell had started a festive blaze in the drawing room fireplace.

The tall case clock in the foyer bonged five times. Mr. O'Dell dropped a cassette in the player, and the solemn chords of a Bach organ prelude resounded through the house. In the drawing room the magistrate was stationed in front of the fireplace. The bridegroom and his best man waited in the foyer. There was a moment of suspense, and then the bride and her attendant appeared on the balcony above and started their dignified descent.

Mrs. Cobb, usually seen in a smock or pantsuit or baggy jumper, was almost stunning in her pink suede suit. Susan Exbridge always looked stunning.

By the time the wedding party lined up in front of the magistrate, he was red faced from the heat behind him. Flanking him on the hearth were two indignant Siamese whose territory in front of the fire was being usurped by a stranger.

Qwilleran felt uneasy; Hackpole fidgeted nervously; and the magistrate mopped his forehead before commencing the brief ritual: "We are gathered together to join together this man and this woman . . ."

Despite the tranquil beauty of the setting, the atmosphere was tense.

"If any person can show just cause why they may not lawfully be joined together, let him now speak or forever hold his peace."

"Yow!" said Koko.

Hackpole frowned; the two women giggled; and Qwilleran felt a mixed reaction of amusement and apprehension.

Herbert took Iris to be his wedded wife, and Iris took Herbert to be her wedded husband. Then it was time for the ring.

This was Qwilleran's moment. The ring was in his pocket, and he fumbled for it. Wrong pocket. Ah! He found the ring. And then he disgraced himself again. The wedding ring flipped out of his hand and rolled down the rug.

Yum Yum was after it in a flash. The resident thief of the Klingenschoen mansion, attracted by anything shiny and gold, batted her small treasure under the Chinese desk with Qwilleran in mad pursuit. Just as the trophy was within his reach, she chased it into the foyer—batting it with one paw, darting after it, batting with the other. She was pushing the ring under an Anatolian rug when the best man finally intercepted it.

At record speed the perspiring magistrate concluded the ceremony. "I pronounce you man and wife." Hackpole gave his bride an embarrassed kiss, and the rest was hugs, handshakes, congratulations, and best wishes.

The buoyant notes of Schubert piano music fitted the occasion, and Mrs. Fulgrove and Mr. O'Dell appeared with trays of champagne and hors d'oeuvres. Qwilleran, with crossed fingers and a glass of white grape juice, proposed a toast to the future happiness of the newlyweds.

The moment of celebration was brief. The magistrate gulped his champagne and left in a hurry, and the new Mrs. Hackpole coaxed her husband into the dining room to see the wild-game carvings on the massive German sideboard.

"I hope she'll be happy," Qwilleran said to Susan Exbridge. "Unfortunately I upheld my reputation as the worst 'best man' in nuptial history."

"But Koko did nobly as best cat," she said. "His well-timed declaration broke the tension."

The Hackpoles returned from their brief sight-seeing and expressed a desire to leave, the groom jingling his car keys and pushing his bride toward the back door.

"Wait a minute," Qwilleran said. "Give me your keys, and I'll bring your car to the front door. We're not throwing rice, but you ought to leave in style."

"But we have two cars," Hackpole objected. "Hers is in the garage."

"Pick it up tomorrow. No one ever heard of a bride and groom leaving in separate vehicles."

Qwilleran and Susan watched them drive away to

the bridal suite in the new Pickax Hotel. "Well, there they go," he said, "for better or worse."

Susan accepted his invitation to dine at Stephanie's, where shaded candles glowed on tables draped to the floor, and soft colors and soft music created a romantic ambience. It was the night before the *Messiah* oratorio, and they discussed the plans for the gala reception at the museum following the performance.

"The Fitch twins are going to do videotapes," Susan said.

Qwilleran nodded his approval. "My friends Down Below refuse to believe the cultural activities in this remote county."

"I consider that we're the Luxembourg of the northeast central United States," Susan said with a dramatic flourish of her expressive hands. "And let me tell you about the surprise we've planned for the *Messiah* audience. Do you know why it's traditional to stand during the 'Hallelujah' chorus?"

"I've heard that the English king was so impressed when he heard it for the first time that he rose to his feet, and when the king stands, everyone stands. Isn't that the legend?"

"That's right! Around 1742. King George the Second will attend the performance tomorrow night, with the entire royal court in eighteenth-century regalia. Our theater group is staging it. . . . You ought to join the Pickax Thespians, Qwill. You have a good voice and a good presence. We could do *Bell, Book and Candle*, and Koko could play Pyewacket."

"I doubt whether he'd want to play a cat," Qwilleran said. "He's an insufferable snob. He'd rather play the title role in *Richard the Third*, I'm afraid."

Dinner with Susan was a pleasant sequel to a wedding he had found distressing. He gave her an armful of pink roses to take home, and she gave him a theatrical kiss. Temporarily he forgot his regret at losing a live-in housekeeper and his disapproval of her choice of husband. He forgot until he made his nightly house check before retiring to his apartment.

A slim volume lay on the library rug. It was a copy of *Othello*, and the best-known quotation came to Qwilleran's mind: *"Then must you speak of one who loved not wisely but too well."*

As he carried the Siamese across the yard in the wicker hamper, he remembered another line, and his moustache bristled. *"Kill me tomorrow; let me live tonight."*

FIFTEEN

Sunday, November twenty-fourth. Two more inches of snow fell during the night. When Qwilleran carried the wicker hamper to the main house on Sunday morning, the bronze bells in the tower of the Old Stone Church and the tape-recorded chimes in the Little Stone Church were announcing morning services. Mr. O'Dell, who had attended early mass, was busy with the snowblower.

"Sure, I'm after clearin' the driveway and parkin' lot for the party tonight," he said. "It won't snow any more today, I'm thinkin'."

Qwilleran turned up the thermostat in the house

and was preparing the cats' breakfast when he heard the back door open and slam shut. It would be O'Dell, he thought, looking for a hot drink on a cold morning. When no one appeared, and when he heard a whimpering in the back hall, he went to investigate.

"Mrs. Cobb!" he exclaimed. "What are you doing here? What's happened to you?"

Her face was haggard and drained of color; her hair was wild; she was leaning weakly against the back door. At the sight of Qwilleran she burst into tears, covering her face with her hands.

He led her into the kitchen and seated her in a chair. "How did you get here? You've been walking in the snow. Where are your boots?"

"I don't know," she wailed. "I just . . . ran out. I had to get away."

"What went wrong? Can you tell me?" He pulled off her wet shoes and bundled her feet in towels.

She shook her head, and a sob turned into a groan. "I've made—I've made a terrible—mistake."

"I don't understand, Mrs. Cobb. Can't you tell me what's happened?"

"He's a monster! I married a monster! Oh, what shall I do?"

"Are you hurt?"

She shook her head, scattering a torrent of tears.

Qwilleran handed her a box of tissues. "Did he abuse you physically?"

"Oh-h-h-h! I can't talk about it!" She put her head down on the table and shook convulsively.

"Was he drinking heavily?"

She managed a tremulous yes.

"I'll make a cup of tea."

"I can't—it won't stay down," she whimpered. "I've been throwing up all night."

"You'd better drink some water, at least. You're probably dehydrated."

"I can't keep it down."

"Then I'm calling the doctor." He dialed the home telephone of Dr. Halifax, and the nurse who took care of the doctor's invalid wife said he was at church.

Qwilleran hurried outdoors and flagged down the houseman. "An emergency, Mr. O'Dell! Rush across to the Old Stone Church and get Dr. Hal. Look for a white head of hair, then walk down the aisle and beckon to him."

"I'll take the snowmobile," Mr. O'Dell said with a puzzled frown.

He roared away on the two-seater, and Qwilleran returned to the kitchen in time to see Koko rubbing against Mrs. Cobb's ankles. When she reached down to touch him, he jumped on her lap. She hugged him, and he allowed himself to be hugged, flicking his ears when her tears fell.

As soon as the noisy machine returned, Qwilleran went to the back door.

"Nice timing," said the old doctor. "You got me out right before they took up the offering. What's the trouble?"

Qwilleran explained briefly and directed him to

the kitchen. In a moment Dr. Hal returned. "Better drive her to the hospital. Where's your phone? I'll order a private room."

"I don't know what it's all about," Qwilleran said in a low voice, "but her husband might be looking for her. I think you should specify no visitors."

He helped Dr. Hal walk the patient to the back door.

"I'll need—some things," she said faintly.

"We'll pack a bag and send it to the hospital. Don't worry about a thing, Mrs. Cobb." Qwilleran would never be able to call her Mrs. Hackpole.

The houseman brought the car up, and Qwilleran said to him, "While I'm gone, would you go to the Little Stone Church and catch Mrs. Fulgrove when the service is over? Ask her to come and pack Mrs. Cobb's personal things for a short hospital stay."

The drive to the hospital was done in silence except for an occasional sob. "I'm so much trouble for you."

"Not at all. You were wise to come back to the house."

When he returned from delivering the patient, Mrs. Fulgrove was bustling about with importance. "I packed all what I could think of," she said, "which it ain't easy seein' as how I never been in hospital myself, God be praised, but I put in what I thought was right and the little radio near her bed, and I looked for a Bible but I couldn't find one, which I packed my own and it should be a comfort to her."

"Had Mrs. Cobb asked you to work tonight during the reception, Mrs. Fulgrove?"

"That she did, but seein' as how it's Sunday—which I don't do work on the Lord's day—I couldn't take money for it, but I'll help out and pleased to do it, seein' as how the poor soul is in hospital and I'm thankful for my health."

Qwilleran asked the houseman to deliver Mrs. Cobb's necessities to the hospital. "Do you think we can manage the reception without her, Mr. O'Dell?"

"Sure an' it's our best we'll be doin'. The club ladies will be after needin' help with the punch bowl and the likes o' that. And should I take the little ones across the yard before the party starts, now?"

"I don't believe so. The cats enjoy a party. Let them stay in the house."

"When the club ladies leave for the concert, I'll be lockin' up and goin' to the church for a little, but I'll be comin' back before it's over. Mrs. Cobb was for turnin' on all the lights and lightin' all the fireplaces. Too bad she won't be enjoyin' it now. What is it that's ailin' herself?"

"Some kind of virus," Qwilleran said.

Around noon the telephone rang, and a thick voice demanded, "Where is she? Where's my wife?"

"Is this Mr. Hackpole?" Qwilleran asked. "Didn't you know? She's in the hospital. She had some kind of attack, they say."

With an outburst of profanity the caller hung up.

Phoning the hospital in the afternoon, Qwilleran learned that the patient was resting quietly and holding her own, but no visitors were permitted, by order of Dr. Halifax.

In the afternoon Susan Exbridge and her committee arrived to prepare the punch and decorate the punch table. At the same moment Polly Duncan arrived with her overnight bag. The women greeted each other politely but not warmly, and the committee seemed surprised to see Polly on the premises.

On the way to the Old Stone Mill for dinner Qwilleran said to Polly, "I see you know Susan Exbridge."

"Everyone knows Susan Exbridge. She's *in* every organization and *on* every committee."

"She thinks I should join the theater group."

"You would find it *very* time-consuming," Polly warned him testily. "If you're serious about writing your book, it would definitely interfere."

She spoke with an acerbity that was unusual for her, and Qwilleran refrained from mentioning Mrs. Exbridge again.

At the restaurant the customers were standing in line, and Hixie was frantically trying to seat the crowd. She had no time for banter. Qwilleran and his guest had to wait for a table and wait for a menu. Judging from the tenor of the conversation in the dining room, everyone was headed for the concert, and everyone was thrilled.

Qwilleran said to Polly, "My mother used to sing in the *Messiah* choir every Christmas. My favorite number is the 'Hallelujah' chorus, especially if they pull out all the stops. I like that two-second rest before the last hallelujah—two seconds of dead silence and then POW!"

Hixie handed them menus with an apology for the delay. Clipped to the folder was a small card suggesting a ready-to-serve Concert Special. Clipped to Qwilleran's menu was another small card scribbled in Hixie's hand: "Want a private talk. Call you tomorrow."

Shortly after six-thirty the restaurant emptied, and the diners converged on the Old Stone Church. The lofty sanctuary was filled to overflowing, both the cushioned pews and the folding chairs in the side aisles. The first three pews were roped off, and the audience was mystified. Guesses and rumors circulated. The anticipation was palpable.

"Do you object to sitting in the back row on the side aisle?" Qwilleran asked Polly. "I want to leave right before the last note, so I can check the museum before the guests arrive."

At seven o'clock Mr. O'Dell slipped into a folding chair nearby, and the two men exchanged nods.

Then the performers appeared—first the orchestra in gray livery. The chorus filed in wearing powdered wigs and pastel costumes—the women in lace fichus and voluminous skirts; the men in knee breeches, waistcoats, and stocks. Finally the soloists made a dramatic entrance in jewel-toned velvets, creating a stir in the audience.

The conductor turned to face the expectant listeners. "Ladies and gentlemen, all rise for His Majesty, King George."

The doors to the rear were flung open, and while the orchestra played coronation music, the royal party moved down the center aisle in dignified procession—a panoply of red velvet, ermine, white satin, and purple damask. The audience gasped, then murmured in wonder, then applauded with delight.

Qwilleran whispered to Polly, "I wish my mother could have seen this. She would have flipped."

The church was noted for its excellent acoustics; the chorus was well rehearsed; the soloists and instrumentalists were professionals; the pipe organ was magnificent. It was a performance Qwilleran would never forget—for more reasons than one.

Toward the end of the oratorio Mr. O'Dell slipped out, giving an explanatory nod to Qwilleran. The orchestra played the opening bars leading up to the first explosive and spine-tingling hallelujah. The king and his royal party rose; the audience rose; and Qwilleran lost himself in the majesty of the music and his own personal nostalgia.

The hallelujahs built up with mounting intensity and joyous celebration, ascending to that dramatic moment—that breathtaking pause—the two seconds of hollow silence!

In that fraction of a fraction of time Qwilleran heard a false note—the wail of a siren. Bruce Scott, seated several rows ahead, slid out of the pew and scuttled up the aisle. Two other men made quick exits. Qwilleran scowled. It was unfortunate timing for the fire siren.

The "Hallelujah" chorus ended, and an aria began.

Then a door behind Qwilleran opened, and an usher tapped his arm and whispered.

Qwilleran was out of his seat instantly, running across the narthex and down the steps. On the other side of the park the museum was aglow—not with light but with a red glare.

"Oh, my God! The cats!" he yelled.

He dashed across the street, dodging traffic. He cut through the park, plowing frantically through deep snow. Flashing red and blue lights surrounded the building. More sirens were sounding.

"The cats!" he shouted.

Black-coated figures were unreeling lines and hoisting ladders. "Stay back!" they ordered.

Qwilleran dashed past them. *"The cats!"* he bellowed.

The red glare spread to the second-story windows. Glass exploded and tongues of flame licked out.

"Stop him!"

He was headed for the back door, nearest the kitchen.

"Keep him out!"

Strong arms restrained him. He looked up and saw the glare spreading to the third floor. Ladders went up. Windows shattered, and black smoke billowed out.

Qwilleran groaned in defeat.

SIXTEEN

Monday, November twenty-fifth. Qwilleran turned on the radio in the bedroom of his garage apartment. "Headline news at this hour: The Klingenschoen Museum on Park Circle was totally destroyed by fire Sunday night, the result of arson, according to fire chief Bruce Scott. A charred body found in the building, allegedly that of the arsonist, has not yet been identified. Thirty fire fighters, four tankers, and three pumpers responded, with surrounding communities assisting the Pickax volunteers. No firemen were injured. . . . We can expect warmer temperatures today and bright sunny skies—"

"Sunny!" Qwilleran muttered, snapping off the radio. He stared with mournful eyes at the gray scene outdoors: the cold, heavy, leaden sky . . . the ground black with frozen mud and soot . . . the smoke-damaged skeleton of a three-story fieldstone building that had once been a showplace. The windows, doors, and roof were gone, and the blackened stone walls enclosed a mountain of charred rubble. The acrid smell of smoke that hung over the ruin also seeped into his apartment.

Polly walked to his side and held his hand in silent sympathy.

"Thank you for helping me get through this ghastly night," he said. "Are you warm enough?" She was wearing a pair of his pajamas. "We didn't get heat until an hour ago. The power came on about five o'clock, but the phone is still dead. The last fire truck didn't leave until daylight."

Gazing at the depressing sight, Polly said, "I can't understand it."

"It's beyond comprehension. Would you like coffee? There's nothing here for breakfast except frozen rolls. What time are you due at the library?"

"YO-W-W-W!" came a loud and demanding howl from the adjoining room.

"Koko heard a reference to breakfast," Qwilleran said as he went to open the door of the cats' parlor.

They walked out with expectant noses and optimistic tails.

"Sorry," he said. "The only aroma this morning is

stale smoke. There's no food until I go to the store. Just be glad you're alive."

"Here comes Mr. O'Dell," Polly said.

"Better go and get dressed."

She grabbed her clothes and disappeared into the bathroom as the houseman plodded up the stairs.

Qwilleran greeted him in a minor key. "It's a sad day, Mr. O'Dell, but we're thankful you saved the cats."

"That boy-o there, it was himself that did it, carryin' on like a banshee an' scratchin' the broom closet door that I waxed only a week since. I opened the door, and it was the picnic basket he was wantin' to get into. Scoldin' the little one, he was, till she jumped in after himself. You were wantin' me to leave them in the house, but it was a divil of a row he was makin', so I carried them over here before goin' to listen to the music a little. A wonder, it is!"

"Koko knew something was going to happen," Qwilleran explained. "He sensed danger. Have you heard anything about the arsonist? On the radio they said he's still unidentified."

"That I did," said O'Dell. "My old friend Brodie I stopped to see this mornin'. It's himself been tryin' to get you on the phone."

"The line has been out of order all night. What did Brodie have to say?"

The houseman shook his head dolefully. "Sure an' I feel sorry for the poor woman—herself in the hospital and her new husband burned to death and a criminal."

Qwilleran was silent. It was the kind of thing that man would do—burn down the museum to stop his wife from working. He was a madman! He was crazy to think he could get away with it.

"I was there when they were after puttin' him in a canvas bag," the houseman said. "It's black, he was, like a burned hot dog, split open and pink inside."

"Spare us the details, Mr. O'Dell. Now it's Mrs. Cobb we have to worry about. We all know how much the museum meant to her."

"Is there anythin' I can do, now, for the poor soul?"

"You can take this money, buy some flowers, and deliver them to the hospital. *Not* pink roses! Wait a minute: I'll write a note to enclose."

The houseman left, and Polly emerged from the bathroom wearing the winter-white dress she had worn to the concert. "This is not what I usually wear for a hard day's work in the stacks," she said. "How can I explain that I lost my luggage in the museum fire?"

"I'm sorry about your luggage, Polly."

"I'm sorriest about those four thousand books."

"It's the library I'll miss most of all," he said. "I saved only one thing. When the auction van delivered the desk, I bribed the porters to bring Mrs. Cobb's wedding present out of the house, so the

Pennsylvania *schrank* is in the garage along with Ephraim Goodwinter's old desk."

The telephone rang, a welcome sound after hours without service. Qwilleran grabbed it. "Yes? . . . It's been out of order, Dr. Hal. What's the situation? . . . That's bad, but there's worse to come. They've identified the arsonist. . . . Would it help if I went to the hospital and had a talk with her? . . . Okay, I'll let you know how it goes."

He replaced the receiver and gazed at it thoughtfully.

"What's the trouble, Qwill?"

"Mrs. Cobb was doing all right until she tuned in her radio and heard the news about the fire. Then it was hysteria-time all over again."

Polly left for work, and the telephone started to ring—and ring. Friends, associates, and strangers called to voice their horrified reactions and offer condolences. Prying busybodies wanted to know who had set the fire—and why. On Main Street a steady stream of motorists cruised around the Park Circle, gawking at the ruins.

Junior Goodwinter's phone call from Down Below came as a surprise. "Qwill! I can't believe it! Jody got a call from Francesca. She said they haven't identified the torch."

"It was Hackpole! One of your own fire fighters."

"Not anymore! They dumped him last spring for infraction of rules. When and if he showed up for training, he was half-shot."

Qwilleran said, "I'm greatly distressed about your mother's accident, Junior. That was a terrible thing."

"Yeah, I know. What can I say?"

"There's been no announcement about the funeral."

"No funeral. I talked to my brother and sister, and we decided to have a memorial service later."

"How will this affect the revival of the *Picayune*?"

"No one knows yet, but I have some good news. You know my dad's fireproof box—it had a key to a vault in Minneapolis. He'd been putting a hundred years of the *Picayune* on microfilm, and he didn't want anyone to know he was spending the money."

"And I have some good news for you," Qwilleran said. "Your great-grandfather's desk is in my garage, and it's yours when you marry Jody."

"Oh, wow!" Junior yelled.

The telephone kept on ringing. Hixie Rice called to inquire if the Siamese were safe and if they needed food. Shortly after, her high-heeled boots were clicking up the stairs, and she delivered a doggie bag of chicken *cordon bleu*.

"I was absolutely *devastated* when I heard about the fire," she said, looking about for an ashtray. "Mind if I smoke, Qwill?"

"Okay with me," he said, "but don't blow smoke at the cats. It'll turn their fur blue."

She pocketed her cigarettes. "I should give them up. They say the damn things cause *wrinkles*."

"Cup of coffee?" Qwilleran suggested.

"If it's your famous instant poison, no thanks."

"Any news about your chef and his knives?"

"Brace yourself," Hixie said. "Did you hear about the unidentified body found in a car stuck in a snowdrift? Well, that was Tony, fleeing to Canada in *my car*!"

"You really know how to pick 'em, Hixie."

"When I told you he escaped through the washroom window, I didn't tell you the whole story. Tony was a French Canadian living here illegally. He changed his name and bleached his hair. I could live with that, but . . . he tried to defraud the insurance company."

"That's bad."

"He sold his car to a chop-shop and reported it stolen. That man was an *insurance* investigator. The first time he came snooping around, Tony took off in the camper and spent a few days in the woods—"

"On *my property*! You told me he'd gone to see his sick mother in Philadelphia. And now what? Does the loss of your partner affect your job?"

"That's what I want to talk to you about, Qwill. My boss was planning a Caribbean cruise with the Goodwinter woman until she decamped with another man and got killed."

"So he wants you to go in her place," Qwilleran guessed.

"Well, he has the reservations and the tickets. . . ."

"Hixie, you're a one-woman true-story magazine. If you're looking for advice, I have no comment to make."

"That's okay. I just wanted to bounce off you. You're so sympathetic."

When Hixie had clicked down the stairs in her pencil-heeled boots, Qwilleran prepared for his visit to the hospital, wondering about Mrs. Cobb's wedding night: Did he threaten to torch the museum? Why didn't she warn us?

He found her sitting in an armchair in her pink robe, staring out the window without her eyeglasses. There were pink carnations and snapdragons on her bedside table, but her radio had been removed. A note propped against the flower vase read: "We miss you—Koko and Yum Yum."

"Mrs. Cobb," he said quietly.

She groped on the windowsill for her glasses. "Oh, Mr. Q! I feel so terrible about everything. I was afraid the cats were trapped in the fire, and I almost died! But now I know they're safe. The flowers are so pretty. I could cry, but I don't have any tears left. When I heard about the museum, I wanted to kill myself! I was sure Herb did it. Did he do it?"

Qwilleran nodded, slowly and regretfully. "The body has been identified. The evidence is all there. I'm sorry to bring you this sad news."

"It doesn't matter. The worst has happened. And I feel so guilty. It's all my fault. Why did I get involved with that man? He did it to spite me—to get his own way."

Qwilleran pulled up a chair and sat down. He spoke gently. "I know it's painful for you, Mrs. Cobb, but no one is blaming you."

"I'll go away when I get out of here. I can live in Saint Louis. I've called my son."

"Don't run away. Everyone likes you. They consider you a valuable asset to the Historical Society and the city. You could open an antique shop—do appraisals—set up a catering business—start a cookie factory. You belong here now."

"I don't have anywhere to go—anywhere to live. That was my *home*."

"I imagine the Goodwinter house will be yours. . . ."

"Oh, I could never live there . . . not after what happened."

"It's Junior's ancestral home. He'd want it occupied by someone like you—with your love for old houses."

"You don't understand. . . ."

Qwilleran's drooping moustache and mournful eyes were compellingly sympathetic. "If you talk about it, you might feel better. Yesterday morning you came trudging through the snow in a weakened condition, after being ill all night. He did something grossly offensive to upset you."

"It was what he *told* me."

Qwilleran knew when to be silent.

"He was drinking. He always got talkative and boastful when he had a few. I didn't mind that."

Qwilleran nodded with understanding.

"He used to tell me about doing heroic things in the army. I didn't believe half of it. But he liked to talk that way, and it did no harm. Once he told me that his father killed Senior's father in a fight, and his uncle helped to lynch Ephraim Goodwinter. He was *proud of it*! I was so stupid! I went along with it and flattered him." She sighed and looked out the window.

"And then . . . on Saturday night at the hotel . . ."

"He started bragging about killing deer out of season . . . overcharging customers . . . cheating on his taxes. He thought that was smart. He said he did the 'dirty work' for XYZ Enterprises. I didn't know what to say. I didn't know whether to believe him." She looked to Qwilleran for approval or disapproval.

He gave a neutral nod and looked encouraging.

"It was my *wedding night*!" she cried in anguish.

"I know. I know."

"Then he told me how his shop did repairs for the Goodwinter cars, and he knew Gritty very well. He kept a bottle in his office and they drank together. Him and a Goodwinter! He seemed to think it was an honor! I guess it's all right to tell you this; she's gone now. They're both gone."

There was a long pause. Qwilleran waited patiently.

After taking a deep breath, Mrs. Cobb said,

"Gritty wanted to get rid of her husband and marry Exbridge, but Senior was broke, and she wouldn't get anything in a divorce. If he died accidentally there would be money from insurance and the sale of the newspaper and antiques and all that."

She had been calm at the beginning, but now she was clenching and unclenching her hands, and Qwilleran said, "Relax and take a few deep breaths, Mrs. Cobb. . . . This is a pleasant room. I had this room when I fell off my bike, but they've changed the hideous wall color."

"Yes, it's a pretty pink," she said. "Like a beauty shop."

"Is the food satisfactory?"

"I haven't any appetite, but the trays look nice."

"The cookies are terrible—take my word for it. They should get a few of your recipes."

She attempted a wan smile.

After a while Qwilleran asked, "Did Herb tell you what actually happened to Senior Goodwinter?"

Mrs. Cobb looked out of the window, then down at her hands. "Senior took his car to Herb's garage for winterizing." Her voice was shaking. "Herb did something to it—I've forgotten what it was—so it would go out of control and burst into flames . . ."

". . . when it hit a bad bump like the old plank bridge?"

She nodded.

"Is that how he bought the farmhouse cheaply?"

She gulped and nodded again.

"And torching the *Picayune* building was part of the deal?"

"Oh, Mr. Q! It was terrible! I told him he was a murderer, and he told me I was a murderer's wife and I'd better keep my mouth shut if I knew what was good for me. He looked terrible! He was going to hit me! I ran in the bathroom and locked the door and got sick. Then he went to sleep and snored all night. I wanted to run away! I got dressed and sat up until morning. When he started to wake up, I ran out of the room—left my wedding suit, purse, everything."

"Then that's how he got the key to the museum."

She groaned, and her face—usually so cheerful—looked drawn and miserable.

When Qwilleran returned to his apartment he opened a can of tuna fish, flaked it, and arranged the morsels on a plain white china plate. "No more home-cooked food," he told the Siamese. "No more gourmet meals. No more antique porcelain dishes."

They gobbled the tuna with heads down and tails up, like ordinary cats. Yet Koko's behavior had been extraordinary. Two hours before the museum fire he had wanted to get out of the building; he *knew* what was coming. What else did he know?

Did he sense that Mrs. Cobb's marriage would end in disaster? How else could one explain his bizarre performance on the pink roses of the rug? And when he uprooted the herb garden, did he perceive some semantic connection with Herb Hackpole? No, that explanation was too absurd even for Qwilleran's vivid imagination. More likely, Koko was simply chewing the leaves as cats like to do, and he got a little high on an herb related to catnip. Yet, they were questions that would never be answered.

Even more perplexing was Koko's attraction to Shakespeare. Could he smell the pigskin covers, or the neat's-foot oil used to preserve the leather, or some rare nineteenth-century glue used in the bindings? If so, why did he concentrate on *Hamlet*?

Koko lifted his head from the plate of tuna and gave Qwilleran a meaningful stare that made his moustache quiver. What was the plot of the play? Hamlet's father had died suddenly; his mother remarried too soon; the father's ghost revealed that he had been murdered; the mother's name was Gertrude.

A shiver ran down Qwilleran's spine. NO! he told himself. The similarity to the Goodwinter tragedy was too fantastic; one could go mad pondering such a possibility. Koko's predilection for *Hamlet* was strictly a coincidence. That, at least, was what he told himself.

The Siamese had finished their dinner and were washing up. The room now smelled of fish as well as acrid smoke. Opening the window a few inches for ventilation, Qwilleran was wounded by the tragic scene outdoors, the ghost of a noble building. Koko had been trying to communicate, and if he had read the cat's meaning, this senseless destruction could have been averted.

What happens next? he asked himself. We can't leave the building in ruins; do we tear it down? The gutted shell was three stories high, solid fieldstone, two feet thick at the base. It occupied a prominent location on Main Street, sharing the Park Circle with the courthouse, public library, and two churches.

Koko jumped to the windowsill, saying "ik ik ik" and wearing a bright-eyed expression of anticipation.

"I'm sorry we haven't had much conversation lately," Qwilleran apologized. "Too many distractions. You probably don't understand the fire and all its ramifications. Will you miss your Shakespeare game? Thirty-seven priceless little books went up in flame. And what shall we do with the remains of the museum?"

As he spoke, it began to snow softly and silently, whitening the frozen ruts and soot-encrusted ice, drawing a merciful white curtain across the ugly scene of devastation.

At the same time Qwilleran slapped his forehead in sudden realization. "I've got it! A theater!" he exclaimed.

"YOW!" said Koko.

"Pickax needs a theater. *'The play's the thing,'* as Hamlet said. We'll have a playhouse, Koko, and you can play Richard the Third. . . . Where are you?"

The cat had vanished.

"Where the devil did that cat go?" Qwilleran thundered with a frown.

Koko had returned to his feeding place and was trying to lick the ceramic glaze from the china plate.

NEW YORK TIMES bestselling author
Lilian Jackson Braun

"Her storytelling voice…is filled with
wonder and whimsy."
—*Los Angeles Times*

First Time in Paperback
The Cat Who Brought Down the House

Actress Thelma Thackeray is organizing a
fundraiser revue starring Koko the cat. But
Thelma's celebration takes an unpleasant turn
when her brother is murdered and Jim Qwilleran
is the suspect. Can Koko put aside stardom
to lend a helping paw in the case?

"Most detectives do their legwork on two legs.
A few, however, do it on four!"
—*Associated Press*

penguin.com